THE LONG SHADOW

Endorsements

Part survival story, part exploration of racial justice in America, part journey of self-discovery, and wholly engaging and memorable. A well done and powerful story. It is certainly stuck in my head.
—Joe Corbett, school librarian, St. Louis

Heartwarming and heartbreaking, Richie's story is a shining example of how taking a chance on unlikely friendships is the best way to break down the barriers we build.
—Jill Williamson, award-winning author of the Blood of Kings trilogy

A powerful message wrapped in a page-turner.
—Cherie Postill, author, speaker, and mentor for teens at the St. Louis Writers Guild

I hope someone out there will read this book, not just those young readers out there but adults as well. This book matters for everyone.
—Mary Kris Rudas, reviewer

I loved this book. I could not stop reading it once I had begun. It is a delightful story, as well as a very painful one, told very well without a wasted word. I gladly recommend it to anyone.
—Jerram Barrs, professor at Covenant Theological Seminary and author of Echoes of Eden: Reflections on Christianity, Literature, and the Arts

In *The Long Shadow*, Richie finds himself traveling through time and learning to explore his own biases and prejudices

towards people of color. Richie's trajectory of self discovery is one that kids of all backgrounds and cultures can enjoy."
—**Rebecca Groves**, middle school literature teacher.

Searching for a new favorite book? Look no further than *The Long Shadow* by Phyllis Wheeler. This is a great book for fans of *To Kill a Mockingbird* but with a time-travel twist. Richie grabs your attention and doesn't let go until the very end.
—**Elsie G**, 13 years old.

Sometimes we need to escape our own time and place to walk a few miles in someone else's shoes. Phyllis Wheeler's *The Long Shadow* will open your eyes, rend your heart, and take you on an invaluable journey.
—**Wayne Thomas Batson**, bestselling author of *The Door Within* Trilogy

Full of interesting characters ... [*The Long Shadow* has] heart, humor, and a great overall theme ... Complex subject matter, woven into enjoyable fantasy ...
—**John Hendrix**, New York Times bestselling illustrator and author

I've read this book and enjoyed the characters in the story. I like the friendship that blossomed in the story and how the story came full circle in the end. It was a good history lesson without being offensive to anyone.
—**LaShaunda Hoffman**, sensitivity reader and autho

This compelling and engaging story is a must read!
—**Rob Currie**, author of *Hunger Winter: A World War II Novel*.

The Long Shadow

Phyllis Wheeler

ELK LAKE PUBLISHING INC

PUBLISHING THE POSITIVE
Plymouth, Massachusetts

COPYRIGHT NOTICE

Cover and Interior Design: Derinda Babcock
Editor(s): Bobbie Temple, Deb Haggerty
Author Represented By: Marit Literary Agency

PUBLISHED BY: Elk Lake Publishing, Inc., 35 Dogwood Drive, Plymouth, MA 02360, 2021

Library Cataloging Data

Names: Wheeler, Phyllis (Phyllis Wheeler)

The Long Shadow / Phyllis Wheeler

202 p. 23cm × 15cm (9in × 6 in.)

Identifiers: ISBN-13: 978-1-64949-131-2 (paperback) | 978-1-64949-132-9 (trade paperback) | 978-1-64949-1333-6 (e-book)

Key Words: Civil rights, black vs white, racism, friendship, relationships, values & virtures, time travel

LCCN: 2021930197 Fiction

DEDICATION

This book is dedicated to the faithful neighbors who shepherded my young white family through our experience living twenty years in a black community. Granny, Ruby, Nonie, Duke: you are in my heart forever.

ACKNOWLEDGMENTS

I want to thank the many writer friends who have encouraged me for years as this project evolved, patiently reading through my manuscript and offering suggestions. I will particularly mention one long-time friend and encourager, LaShaunda Hoffman, who as a Missouri African-American and a writer has read the book and given me extremely valuable feedback. A partial list of writer friends who helped includes Rebekah Larson, Neil Das, Ellen Parker, Terri Proksch, Laura Schmidt, Jan Davis Warren, Jody Feldman, and Rachel Hauck.

My husband Steve has been an invaluable support to me in this long journey.

I am also indebted to my publisher, Deb Haggerty; my editor, Marcie Bridges; and my agent for this book, Bob Shuman, for his encouragement and his razor-sharp editing skills.

I am indebted to Doug Hunt, a retired professor at the U. of Missouri who in 2010 published a book about the lynching, Summary Justice: The Lynching of James Scott and the Trial of George Barkwell in Columbia, Missouri, 1923. I also drew heavily on the work of Jason Jindrich, who wrote a master's thesis in 2002 at Mizzou about historical conditions in the black neighborhoods in Columbia, and I read plenty of other studies and newspaper articles.

CHAPTER 1

Weather was brewing. Heat was still rising from the pavement when the wind started up, carrying with it the tang of coming rain. Gray clouds rumbled overhead, and I broke into a jog through Shady Creek's century-old downtown.

That's when an old man ran straight into me—or maybe I ran into him. His silver pocket watch left his grip and went flying, and he grabbed me to steady himself with a feeble dark-skinned hand. We both stared as the watch dropped to the sidewalk and cracked open, spilling its guts.

I shook my head. He didn't have a phone—he had a pocket watch. This guy was from a different century, a really different century. "I'm sorry," I said. "I was going too fast. Didn't see you." I knelt, face to the wind to get the curls out of my eyes, and took a baker's minute to pick up a handful of tiny parts.

He seemed frail, hunched over a wooden cane. He looked at the watch pieces in my hand and murmured, "It was my grandad's." Then his eyes roved over to my face.

"Richie." He said my name as if he knew me.

Now that was pretty freaky. He couldn't know my name because we'd never met.

"Richie," he whispered.

Tingles spidered up my back. I could count the African-Americans I knew by name on one hand, and none of them carried pocket watches.

"I'm really sorry, sir," I babbled. "I hope you can get the watch fixed. I just spent my money—" I thrust the pieces into his hand.

I heard rapid footsteps and looked up. Three black teens came from the general direction of a nearby store. Two of them wore black hoodies. I sucked in my breath. This was precisely the type of situation my dad had warned me about. "Don't go where there's a crowd of black people."

"Pops!" said one. "You all right?"

"Sure I am," said the old man.

The tallest guy stared daggers at me.

I didn't know what he wanted, but I ran anyway as the rain began to pelt me. Ran like my life depended on it, and maybe it did.

Danger, right here in Shady Creek, Missouri, my mostly white, boring suburb. Who would have thought?

———◆●◆———

I won't josh you. The last couple years of my life were tough. I'd gone from a normal kid with two loving parents to a kid raised by his mean aunt—somebody who I guess never wanted children, especially not now.

I missed Dad, that was for sure. Mom too. Same town, same friends, different house. But it felt like different everything. Like there was a big gaping hole inside of me. I did my best to carry on, keep Dad's advice in my head, cooperate most of the time.

I'd have left Aunt Trudy's if I could. But I was only fourteen. How can a fourteen-year-old leave? I had to figure it out. Not that my dad would approve. "You can't run away from trouble," he used to say, tapping his finger on his bearded chin. "It'll always find you."

I didn't believe what Dad said. Getting out of Shady Creek was my number one goal.

After two years living with Aunt Trudy, I even believed her sometimes when she said I did everything wrong. But not today. Despite the puzzling encounter with the old man, today I was Smiling Sam, Tall Teddy, Rich Richie. This afternoon I'd be out of town, all the way out to the woods where I was good at things. Even if it wasn't for very long, it would still be something. Just a little orienteering session while Aunt Trudy was at work, now that school had let out for the summer.

After the storm passed, it only took another hour before me and Ethan made our way out to the Scout troop's borrowed woodlands. A battered "No Trespassing" sign hung over the warm, shady clearing, nailed to one of the oak trees.

We weren't supposed to be here unless we were with the Scout troop. But the troop wasn't meeting this summer since the leadership was changing. Of course, I couldn't stay away. I was drawn to the woods like a bat to the twilight sky.

Besides, nobody would notice. Mrs. O'Rourke, who owned the property, was deaf as a post. Probably blind too.

We pulled out our compasses and a map. I opened the folded-up instructions for orienteering. Ethan leaned forward, dark hair falling into his eyes, hands on knees, and gazed at the paper in my hand. "I don't remember much."

"The target is right there on the map," I explained. "All we have to do is lay the map flat, turn the compass on the map so the north arrow on the compass matches the north arrow on the map, and then head out in the direction of the target."

"Oh, yeah." He slapped his forehead. "I remember now."

We laid the compass on top of the map, sitting in the palm of Ethan's hand, and gazed off in the indicated direction toward a wooded hillside.

"It's a paint mark on a tree, right?" Ethan squinted. "Black?"

"Yup. I bet the paint marks are still here. It hasn't even been a year since we did orienteering with the troop. Here in this very spot."

Walking a straight line through woods isn't particularly easy. You gotta dodge around trees and thickets and stuff like that. And a black paint mark isn't easy to find. But we were doing our best.

After a while, we came to an ancient barbed-wire fence. A property boundary?

"I think we should have found that marker by now," said Ethan.

He was right. "Oh man," I said.

Ethan laughed. "You always say that."

I shrugged. "Let's try again. Like my dad always said—"

"Patience, persistence, perseverance." He finished the sentence for me, and I punched him in the arm.

We headed back to where we'd started. I picked up a walking stick and whacked a dead tree with it. It made a satisfying sharp crack.

A dog on the other side of the hill started barking.

We looked at each other and walked faster.

An engine started on the other side of the hill and growled closer.

I froze. Ethan's eyes opened wide.

It sure did sound like a truck rumbling in our direction on the gravel road. The gravel road that was supposed to be our way home.

We crashed through the dense brush under a tree while an ancient, rusted Ford pickup slowly drove past.

The driver stopped the vehicle. Opened the door. And got out. A huge man, wearing overalls and a plaid shirt. "You! Get over here!" His voice rumbled like a volcano.

We crumpled the map and took off running, dodging leaves and branches. "The caretaker. For Mrs. O'Rourke," Ethan gasped.

My heartbeat thundered in my ears.

Up ahead, a small black and white animal blindly stumbled into a stump, just his head covered by an empty tuna can.

The little skunk needed help. But we needed to keep going.

"C'mon!" Ethan, panting beside me, pulled on my sleeve. "Leave him alone!"

Footsteps stomped through leaves behind us.

Did I dare help the little guy? If I didn't, who would?

I changed direction, reached down as I dashed past, snagged the can, and then dropped it. I held my breath for a second, even with my legs pumping like crazy, and then let it out. He hadn't sprayed me.

The footsteps behind us stopped. Maybe the skunk was positioning himself to defend his rescuers, and our pursuer didn't want to test him. Relief washed over me. I glanced over at Ethan and grinned as we pounded a shortcut to the blacktop road without pursuit.

Dodging vines and bushes, we made it to the edge of the road where we flopped down, panting.

Once we had settled down, Ethan stood and started back toward town. "Come on, let's get out of here."

We pocketed our compasses and folded up the map, then sauntered along for a while, catching our breaths. We pretended to look cool, and then we started laughing like crazy. No. We had to be calm and collected. In case a police cruiser came by.

But we just couldn't stop laughing.

THE LONG SHADOW

Flashing its lights, a vehicle pulled up next to us silently. "You kids, get over here."

Busted.

CHAPTER 2

Aunt Trudy picked me up at the police station. I had to wait alone in a small room with a battered desk and a couple of metal chairs till she got off work. Long after Ethan's mother took him home.

Aunt Trudy glared at me and shook her wiry brown hair. "Trespassing. Of all things, Richie. You're fourteen years old. You know better than this."

"Yes, ma'am." I adopted a monotone voice and stared at the floor. The best way, I'd discovered, to keep her from blowing her stack. But sometimes it backfired.

She stamped her foot. "I don't know why you do these things. Sneaking around with your friends while you're supposed to be at home. Now, trespassing. Next, it will be stealing. Yes, I do know why you do these things. You're stupid and lazy and disobedient too. I don't know what my brother kept seeing in you."

Man, I missed him. Why did he and Mom have to be in that car accident? I needed them bad along about now.

"In fact, I'm ready to give up," Aunt Trudy said, her hands on her hips now. "I'm calling the Family Support Division in the morning. You're going somewhere else. I don't know what they could have expected me to do."

I felt like someone socked me in the gut. "Where?"

"Wherever they've got for trespassers like you. For delinquent boys like you."

I pulled myself up to my full height. "I don't want to live with you either," I said.

"I'll bet." She marched out of the room and motioned for me to follow. The ride home was silent. My thoughts drifted to other car rides, Mom at the wheel, chatting with me about my day and telling me what a good job I was doing at the target range.

Before I got out of the car, Aunt Trudy said, "You'll learn."

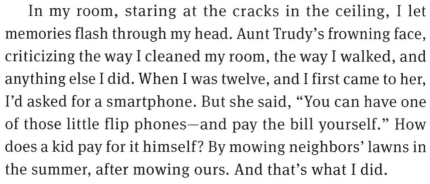

In my room, staring at the cracks in the ceiling, I let memories flash through my head. Aunt Trudy's frowning face, criticizing the way I cleaned my room, the way I walked, and anything else I did. When I was twelve, and I first came to her, I'd asked for a smartphone. But she said, "You can have one of those little flip phones—and pay the bill yourself." How does a kid pay for it himself? By mowing neighbors' lawns in the summer, after mowing ours. And that's what I did.

The Ozarks called to me, troops and troops of green hills marching into the distance filled with oak and pine and squirrels. A calm, quiet place where no one could bother me. That would be just fine.

But how would I get there?

Aunt Trudy probably meant to ground me for the weekend, but she was so focused on sending me to live somewhere else she hadn't said the words. Ethan, Jack, and Ethan's brother were still coming by in the morning, after she left for work, to pick me up for camping, despite the little scrape with the law.

Then, I'd just … stay in the woods after they left. I'd never see this new "home" she was going to dig up for me. It was probably juvie, or some kind of detention center. Even though the extent of my crimes consisted only of a record of bad grades in the past two years and the trespassing incident.

No to juvie. Or anywhere else someone dreamed up. I had to leave if I wanted to get control over my life.

I could live in the woods. I'd been a Scout a while, and my dad taught me stuff, like how to shoot my modest .22-caliber rifle. I could cook. I could fish. I could forage.

I could do it. I could strike out on my own.

I packed up my camping gear in my big camping backpack, my super big box of ammo Dad had bought me, my edible plants book, some changes of clothes, four Pop-Tarts, three cheese sandwiches, and my phone. I put a picture of my mom and dad in a side pocket. That's all I needed.

CHAPTER 3

We had a great weekend. "Have a nice trip back." I sat down on the rock next to the campfire. Ethan and Jack, wearing their backpacks, were ready to go back to Shady Creek with Ethan's brother who waited in the car out at the road.

Ethan lifted an eyebrow. "You're coming, right?"

I hesitated. I didn't like being alone. A Scout always has a buddy. What was I risking?

Stupid. Idiot. Aunt Trudy's words flowed through my mind like toxic sludge. And the kicker: *You're going somewhere else.*

I was good at living in the woods. A good shot. I had lots of know-how. I could even use a compass.

I stood up. "I can't go back. I gotta try it out here."

Jack frowned. "Our food is all gone."

"There's plenty of water here. I can fast one day, no problem. If I can't make it, I'll call."

Jack wagged a finger at me. "You don't have a buddy. Scouts always have a buddy."

"Here's my buddy." I picked up my rifle.

Ethan shrugged. "Okay, suit yourself." He turned toward the road. "You're keeping the tent."

Jack and Ethan started down the path. Jack stopped and turned. "I don't feel real good about this."

I shooed them away . "Go, just go. It's what I want. I just need some space."

Jack sighed, letting his shoulders droop. "All right." He straightened up. "So, what do I tell your aunt?"

"Aw, just tell her I can take care of myself. You know it's true."

Jack nodded.

The leaves rustled under their feet as they left.

I watched them go, holding my breath to keep the loneliness out of my chest. After they left my line of sight, I started breathing again. I listened to the faint creaking of the wind in the trees. I was alone. Completely alone.

And hollow inside.

I bent down and tried to open the cattail roots we'd collected. There wasn't much edible—too early in the growing season. I'd have to count on shooting a rabbit, making rabbit stew tonight. I fed the tiny fire the remains of the cattail roots. The fire spat and sparked in response, keeping the silence at bay.

First thing Aunt Trudy might do when they got back was send somebody out looking for me. She might be secretly relieved I'd left town. But she wouldn't want the neighbors to think she was a bad parent, so she'd call the cops on me, for sure.

Ethan and Jack would probably be home in an hour or so, and they knew just where I was.

I needed to move camp.

CHAPTER 4

I kicked dirt to kill the fire and tied my sleeping bag to my backpack. In one hand, I picked up the gun, in the other the tent bag. My footsteps crunched the gravel on the road as I made my way down to the highway.

I needed to be somewhere else. Anywhere else.

I started walking away from St. Louis. A few cars whizzed past. The sun beat down, and I took a long drink from my water bottle.

Was that a cop car coming? I dodged off the road and hid in some bushes.

A wave of nausea hit me. Not only that, but someone's face flashed before me, then was gone. My skin tingled.

Was I sick? For some reason, there were dead leaves lying around my feet I hadn't noticed before. In fact, they were everywhere. I needed to clear my mind.

A few old cars whizzed past. Maybe there was an antique car show down in Farmington. Knowing all about antique automobiles was a hobby I'd shared with Dad, and now it was part of my way of proving to myself I wasn't stupid. But for shows, the classic cars were all polished up. Mostly, these weren't. Odd.

Fall leaves? Antique cars? I could swear I'd stepped into an old movie of the 1950s or 60s. But no, that couldn't be.

I took a long drink from my bottle that was half empty already, even though the day wasn't that hot—at least not as hot as yesterday. I kept walking, holding my gun and my tent.

I wasn't getting anywhere fast on foot. Maybe I needed to try hitchhiking. I knew that was dangerous, not the thing to do and everything, but I really didn't want the cops from Shady Creek to find me so close to last night's campsite. And I knew people still hitchhiked out here in the country where no one had much money. Dad and I had even picked someone up once. So, I stuck my thumb out as I walked and said a little prayer. Maybe God was there. Maybe he heard me.

Soon I heard rumbling behind me as an old green box truck pulled over. It was much bigger than a pickup, large enough to move and haul commercially. The truck needed a paint job, that's for sure, not to mention looking crazy old and out of style with its rounded fenders. A sign on the side of the box read "Wizer's Pasta," the gold letters arranged in an arch. I didn't recognize the name at all.

The driver gestured from his window. "Climb in," he said in a welcoming voice. "I'm headed south."

Was I safe? I eyeballed him. Close-cropped kinky white hair. Light-brown skin the color of coffee with cream. A round face, a broad nose, an apologetic grin. He didn't seem like someone out to do bad things to hitchhikers.

Dad had hitchhiked some in his youth when it was more common. The truckers, he'd said, were the ones to ride with. They just wanted to pass the time of day.

I showed the gun to him. "Okay if I bring this?"

"Sure. Going camping?"

"Yeah."

For country people, a gun was a necessity, something you needed to put food on the table. So different from attitudes in the city.

I climbed into the passenger side of the cab, where ringing trumpets pealed from the speakers and sent a thrill up my spine, even though I wasn't into that kind of music. I liked hip-hop.

There was room, barely, to fit my stuff on the floor of the cab and on the bench front seat. I sat gingerly between the backpack and sleeping bag, wedged the gun in next to the door, and looked out the window, wondering why he was listening to this. But somehow I didn't think he'd hurt me or take me somewhere I didn't want to go.

The driver shoved the gearshift forward. He had a bit of a tummy on him, and he wore a sleeveless undershirt that displayed heart-shaped tattoos on his arms. "It's a warm day. Odd for this time of year," he said.

"This time of year?" It was June. I tugged at the neckline of my tee shirt. "I like it warm."

As we drove along, I noticed there weren't just a few fall leaves. The whole landscape had taken on an orange tint. At least, the leaves had. In fact, most of them had fallen off the branches.

"What's the deal with the falling leaves?" I asked.

"You surprised? Life can be full of surprises," he said.

I frowned. "I'm surprised, all right. Why doesn't it look like June?"

He raised an eyebrow and shook his head, like he didn't know the answer. "Sometimes we just have to face life with the heart of a poet," he said. "Take the surprises as they come."

"Poet?"

"Sure. Here's my haiku for the day." He spouted off a few words that talked about falling leaves and hope.

I didn't know what to say. I didn't remember much about haiku, except that it's Japanese poetry, and you count syllables to write one.

A 1960s-era Chevy swished by, going the opposite direction. "I'm seeing a lot of antique cars today," I said. "What's that?" I pointed.

He shrugged, white eyebrows lifting, and smiled. "An old truck."

What did I expect him to say? He wasn't Dad, that was for sure. Dad would have known.

Similar traffic passed us. Chevys, Fords, Buicks from the fifties and sixties.

A singer wailed from the radio about a lost love. "Teen Angel."

"Hey, you believe in angels?" asked the trucker.

"Not me." Silly topic. If angels were for real, they hadn't helped me out.

Miles fell away under the tires. My stomach started to feel better, and my hands, clutching my water bottle strap, relaxed. My leg stopped jiggling. The warm air blowing in through the window smelled of musty leaves and, oddly, cinnamon.

The vibration of the road lulled me. I dozed off.

When I woke up, the sky had clouded over, and my throat felt dry. We were driving past some woods. I drank most of the rest of the water in my plastic bottle.

The trucker turned the music down. "We're fifteen minutes from Farmington. The camping might be good around here."

A good spot, then. "Here," I said. "Please stop here."

He pulled over. I hoisted my pack and other belongings over my shoulder.

"You make a habit of camping solo?" he asked.

"It's one of those things where the young brave goes out into the wilderness by himself for a while," I said. I sounded a lot more confident than I felt.

"I see." He gave me a knowing look.

"I'll be fine." He might have a grandkid my age, who knew? "Maybe you'll pick me up next time you come through here," I said. "Maybe you'll have another haiku for me."

The trucker tossed me a Twinkie and a plastic-wrapped sandwich. "Take these."

A whiff of cinnamon tickled my nose, again. Where did that come from?

The sandwich looked brown and wrinkly. Made with heels. Not my favorite. Maybe I even made a face.

He shook his head. "You need to learn to live outside your comfort zone," he said.

I needed the food. "Right. Thanks." After he let me out, I watched the truck putter on down the road. For some reason, I felt sad he was gone.

CHAPTER 5

Piles of orange, yellow, and brown leaves lay around my feet, and many bare branches hung above my head. The cool afternoon breath of the woods felt like fall.

But it was June.

I dug into my backpack and found my phone. Cell service wasn't working, even though I'd paid the bill. Maybe I was too far out in the country. Maybe Aunt Trudy cut it off. Or maybe I was just lost in time, ha ha. Good. Then Aunt Trudy and the cops in Shady Creek would never find me.

I took a deep breath through my nose, savoring. This was what freedom smelled like—minty pine and dusty leaves. I was free, and I was in my element, in the woods. That was all that mattered.

I was chilly. I fished my jacket out of my backpack. Good thing I brought it.

I was certainly hungry. After only a moment of hesitation, I gobbled the trucker's sandwich as I strolled along a deer trail. It turned out to be ham and cheese, hefty and hearty—and I managed to ignore the heels. After half a mile, I chose a clearing where I could still faintly hear the occasional rumbling of vehicles passing on the road. No sense getting lost. Taking my time, I put up the tent beneath a giant oak that dominated the forest around it, on a slight incline for good drainage, and then finished off the Twinkie.

For my new home in the woods, it would do very well. I puffed out my chest and sent a fist pump toward the sky.

But the sky had changed. The glare of the sun had given way to a cool wind that shoved gray clouds together, covering what had been blue.

In the distance, the sky rumbled.

Rain. One thing I hadn't counted on.

I needed water. Hastily I put the gun and my pack inside the tent, covered it with the sleeping bag, and zipped the flaps shut. Then I set out to find a stream. I kept walking downhill. I turned left at a lonely boulder, right at a fallen log, walked downhill, and walked downhill some more until I found a tiny creek flowing with tea-colored water, stained by fallen leaves.

Well, tea-colored was better than no water. I filled the bottle and took a sip.

Somewhat bitter. But drinkable. I drank deeply and refilled it.

The sky rumbled again, louder.

Now to find the tent again. In the dim light, everything looked the same. Would the orange tent stand out? I started walking uphill. I didn't realize how far down I'd come. Turned left at the fallen log. Right at the lonely boulder. It was getting darker. More rumbling. Louder.

Rain was coming. My hands grew clammy. I needed to find shelter.

Brambles clawed at my hands and my clothing.

I didn't remember any brambles.

Lightning flashed. A searing crack of thunder chased it by less than a second.

Out in the storm, no tent. Why had I thought getting water right now was so important?

Don't stand under a tree in a thunderstorm. I'd heard that so many times. But now I had no choice.

Hail the size of peas clattered through the branches. Wind tried to shove me over. I moved to the leeward side of a large tree and stood under a limb. A tree not far away toppled with a crash. Branches lashed and groaned, whipped around by an unseen force. I squatted, head down, arms up. Hail stung my exposed hands and forearms.

Next came driving rain that soaked me instantly. More lightning flashes, more nearby crashes of thunder. I shuddered and shivered.

My body trembled like a mad dog's. I couldn't take more of this. I needed to leave, get some help, hitchhike home. I crouched there, overwhelmed with the need to flee—and unable to.

I calmed myself with deep breaths as I rubbed my arms. Maybe I could generate some heat that way. Tough it out.

Eventually the wind died down, and the rain kept falling. I stood up and brushed the water out of my eyes, relief washing over me. I was still alive.

I really wasn't sure which way I should go. The tent had to be nearby. I jumped up and down to keep warm, bobbing under the broad tree limb until the thunder receded into the distance and the rain stopped.

I could still see my hands. Barely.

All I had was my water bottle. I took a sip of the pungent tea. The taste of freedom. My lips quivered with cold.

In my head, I began retracing my steps. I'd walked the long way up, made the turns, and then I'd run into the brambles. I needed to go back through the brambles. In the dimness, with hands extended in front of me, I groped until I found the briar patch. I gingerly walked through, unhooking thorns from my clothing, and turned up the hill.

A pitch-black wall loomed in front of me. I reached out and touched it. Rough, wet, crumbling rock greeted my fingers. I stood at the foot of a limestone formation, maybe a cliff.

I'd never been here before.

"No!" I smacked the rock wall. "I can't be lost!" The sound of my cracking voice echoed against the cliff wall.

I kicked the wall. It felt good, so I kicked it again.

Some woodsman I was, making foolish decisions. I started shivering again. When I kicked the wall this time, it hurt.

I could only see black.

I might be dead by morning, found at the foot of the cliff, curled up and cold.

I turned around, back to the cliff, and opened my eyes wide, but the velvety blackness revealed no secrets. My body shivered violently now.

Maybe there was a tree to my left. Maybe not.

I knew I had to keep moving to stay warm enough. It was as simple as that.

I started hopping up and down. After a minute, I felt warmer.

Water drops made splatting sounds as they fell from the trees in the wind. I hopped and tried to think of warm things. A nice, warm campfire. A beach. Lying in the summer sun. Summer didn't seem real now.

"Yo!" A voice called from somewhere. "Somebody out there?"

Silence. Then I shouted, "Yes."

The bobbing light of a flashlight appeared in the blackness a hundred feet away, along the foot of the cliff. "You lost?" The rich bass voice held a deep country accent.

"Don't know what happened ..." My voice cracked.

"You a kid?"

"Fourteen."

Footsteps shuffled through sodden leaves.

I walked toward the light, one hand on the rough rock wall.

I stopped. The light blinded me for a moment and then traveled down my soaked jacket and jeans. My hand clutched the water bottle that hung from a strap over my shoulder.

"What you doin' out here?" said the voice.

I squinted and shook my head. "Camping."

"You can't camp out here in cold weather, unless you know what you're doing."

The light paused on the ground and then, held at arm's length, slowly moved up the form of the man, wearing jeans, a red flannel shirt, and finally illuminating his dark face

I let go of the water bottle. It sloshed against my side.

"You want to live, boy, you need to come with me." The man shook his head, turned around, and started back the way he came.

I stood frozen. Who was this man?

Did I follow him?

Fear washed over me. Fear of the man. Fear of staying behind, freezing to death. I had to choose.

"You're gonna freeze out here." He'd turned his head to fling the words over his shoulder.

The bobbing light was getting smaller. Leaving me behind.

If I didn't follow, I knew I didn't have much chance to make it. Fear of that propelled me forward, bigger than my fear of anything else.

It was a chance to live.

CHAPTER 6

I scrambled up the dark cliff behind the man, feeling for hand holds.

On a shelf ten feet above the ground, the man began shining his flashlight back and forth ahead of him, revealing a shallow cave and, inside it, a tiny encampment. "Set yourself down, stay a while." His voice rumbled, like he hadn't used it lately. "It's been a long time since I talked."

I stumbled toward the only place to sit, a stool, where I huddled and shivered.

The man draped a blanket around my shoulders. "I'll have a fire going in a minute."

He knelt and picked up wood and kindling, which he tossed into a pile. Soon flames licked upward and outward toward the cave's mouth, casting reddish light and giving off the aroma of wood smoke.

"Water?" The man offered a chipped brown coffee mug filled with liquid.

"Ah, no thanks. I'll drink mine." I couldn't help grimacing at the taste from my bottle.

"You got that from the creek down the hill."

"Yep."

"There's a nice river. Farther away, though."

"Ah."

The man was tall, broad-shouldered. Not an old man. Dreadlocks framed his face. He wiped his right hand on his pants and extended it. "Name's Morris."

"Richie." I shook hands, feeling my freezing hand lost in the massive warm grip.

"What brings you out here?"

Might as well try to say it like it was. "My aunt wants to send me away to juvie, so I ... thought I'd better make it on my own."

Morris knelt and set a coffeepot on the grate over the fire. "You don't look like a juvenile delinquent."

"I'm not a juvenile delinquent." I drew the blanket closer. "I need to learn to shoot a rabbit with my .22. Cook it. Eat it. So I can stay in the woods."

"Right."

Morris shuffled to the other side of the cave opening and peered out, looking like he lost something. He turned back. "You tried shooting rabbits before? It ain't easy."

"I'm a good shot. My dad taught me."

Morris threw a log onto the fire, and it flared bigger.

I looked around at the sparse belongings neatly arranged. The top shelf of a wire rack held a cooking pot, a few utensils, and three old-fashioned canteens. A bowl full of nuts occupied the bottom shelf, alongside a tin of Maxwell House coffee. Against the rock wall leaned an axe, probably for chopping wood. I wasn't ready to call him an axe murderer yet.

It was just a few steps to the bedroll against the rock wall. He didn't have much room. "I hunted for a rabbit earlier. Didn't see one though."

"Where's your gun? Your stuff?" Morris poked the fire, sending sparks toward the mouth of the cave.

"Before it rained, I put the tent up, put the stuff in it."

"You don't know?"

"It's around here somewhere. Could even be close."

Morris nodded in the direction of what might be called a corner. Leaning against the wall, glimmering in the flickering light, was a rifle, partially wrapped in a blanket. "That's how I'll get me a deer in deer season. You ever try that?"

"No, sir. And the rest of the time?"

Morris shrugged. "Go fishing. Shoot rabbits."

"You know about plants to eat?"

"Sure. Been eatin' persimmons lately. Jerusalem artichoke, there's a good one."

I stood up, started pacing, and stopped short at the back of the cave. Morris was shooting rabbits, eating persimmons, and all that. Maybe he could show me some things I'd like to know. "Hey, do you eat cattails?"

Morris snorted. "Naw. It's a lot of work for just a few bites that don't hold you." He walked over to the wire shelf and found a bowl of nuts. "But I know what to do to acorns so I can eat 'em. Go ahead. Give it a try." He held out the bowl.

I knew better than that. "No, thanks."

"I soak them in the river for days and then boil 'em for a while, and that poison stuff goes away." He held out the acorns again. "Try it."

"No, thanks."

I should leave. I didn't like eating poisonous things.

Wind shuffled the tree limbs outside the cave with creaking and groaning.

"Suit yourself."

I still shivered and sat again on the stool. Winter was coming on. I didn't believe it, but it seemed to be true. "You going to be here all winter?"

"Been here two winters already. This will be my third."

Morris began sharpening his axe with a whetstone he pulled from his pocket. He had a small smile on his face.

The noise his work made filled the cavern like the sound of hornets on guard.

Goosebumps raised on my forearms.

After five minutes, he put the stone away and stood the axe against the wall. In spite of myself, my exhausted body relaxed.

Morris fed the fire, stirred it, and eventually let it die down. Its crackling voice turned into a whisper, and its yellow glow turned to faint red. We stared at the fire without talking. I really didn't know if I was asleep or awake.

He offered me the bedroll and took the blanket around his own shoulders. Morris stood by the cave entrance and peered out into the damp, windy night as I nestled into the bedding.

I couldn't trust him. But I had to.

CHAPTER 7

The scent of coffee brewing woke me. Dim daylight lit the rock wall in front of me, as if from a far window. At first, I didn't know where I was.

"You awake?" He was sitting on the stool, and moved the gray enamel coffeepot over a few inches on the grate over the fire.

"Yeah. I suppose so." I sat up and then looked around at the back of the cave. Only the bedroll, the stool, and the fire grate holding the coffeepot remained.

"Sometimes it's damp in here. That bed ain't got no soft mattress, either." Morris sipped from a mug. "You want some coffee?"

I pulled myself up out of the bedroll. "Don't like it," I said, although I'd never actually had it. The stuff looked a lot like mud to me, smelled even worse. I glanced at the cave opening. The rays of sunlight reached downward, not sideways. I realized the sun had been up for some time.

"I got nothing else to offer you, if you ain't goin' to eat acorns." Morris stood and retrieved the bowl. He popped a handful into his mouth and crunched. "But acorns fill you up pretty good." He waved it in my direction. "Want some?"

I came closer and decided to take one. The smooth nuts, minus their little hats, looked a lot like hazelnuts. "What do you do to them?"

"Soak 'em in a stream for days and days, and boil 'em for one day. That gets that bitter taste out. Then I crack the shells off."

Morris had just eaten some himself. It tasted a lot like any other nut, actually. I chewed on a couple more. They really weren't so bad. "They never taught us this in Scouts."

Morris laughed. "Remember, it takes days and days to fix 'em. Probably too long for the Scouts."

The cave looked different now. Most of Morris's sparse belongings had been moved and stacked near the opening.

"I missed the hunting hour for rabbits already this morning."

"Gotta get up before dawn for that."

"Or do it in the evening." I was guessing.

Morris nodded. "Well, I got to get moving, Richie. You need to go on back to your tent. I found it, thirty yards that way." He nodded toward the rising sun. "Now, I want you to do something for me."

"Sure."

"Anybody asks if you met anybody, you tell 'em no."

"Uh, okay ...?"

"Because somebody's going to come looking for you, and then they are going to find me, and I don't want 'em to." Morris reached for his gun. "Time for me to move on, anyways."

Guilt tugged at me. I didn't want Morris to leave the safe, warm shelter of the cave on account of me. "Where else you going to go?" I took another handful of acorns and threw them into my mouth.

"Further into the woods. I'll find me a spot. I been in this cave a couple of years, and I can't tell if somebody might have seen me, anyways."

I rolled up the bedroll tight and laid it on top of the other belongings.

Then Morris walked to the back of the cave and picked up a bit of silvery paper. A gum wrapper from my pocket. The big man shook his dreadlocks and started back toward his pile of stuff, jaw set.

Picking up my trash, it was too much. I stumbled to my feet, stepped forward, and stood in front of him, blocking his way. "Nobody's coming after me."

"Sure they are."

"No. I hitchhiked away from home, didn't know the guy who gave me a ride."

Morris stopped and looked at me, balancing on both feet like a cat. "Your friends don't know where you is at?"

"That's true."

"But you did hitchhike out here."

"Right."

"What kind of ride you get?"

I scratched my head. "An old guy, white hair. He gave me something to eat."

Morris kicked the remains of the fire. "Does he know your name?"

"No."

"He knows you are from Shady Creek?"

"No." Morris seemed to know Shady Creek. "You from Shady Creek, Morris?"

He surveyed me without smiling and said nothing.

Was he angry now?

He let out a deep breath and turned to his rope-entwined pile of belongings. He grunted as he pulled out a long stick and turned to me. "I need to go fishing."

"Look, nobody's gonna look for me."

"That's why I'm asking you. I need to go fishing. You coming?"

I closed my eyes. I really should high-tail it out of here while I could.

I told him I needed to check my campsite.

CHAPTER 8

A thick limb had fallen on my tent and collapsed it. What if I hadn't made my trip to get water? When it started raining, I would have crawled into the tent.

I shuddered. It was like an unseen hand had moved me to a safe spot at the foot of the cliff, cold and wet as it was. And brought me help.

The poles were bent but not broken. I straightened them out. The tent could still be my home.

I hung the sleeping bag from a tree limb and made a rough clothesline out of my rope, long enough for all the tee shirts, jeans, sweatshirt, and socks.

It would take a while for all this to dry.

I sat down and cleaned my gun, making sure it wouldn't rust. The ammo looked sealed, so the gunpowder probably still worked. The gun ought to bring down a rabbit for me— tonight for sure. It was a good thing I'd practiced a lot, with Dad and with the Boy Scouts. After all, Dad used to tell me, "Be persistent. It's the only way you'll learn to shoot straight."

I crashed around in the brush nearby until I found a long straight piece of stiff woody vine that would do nicely as a fishing pole, and began sawing away at one end of it with my pocketknife.

"Need some help?" Morris appeared from nowhere. He pulled out his large knife and clipped off the end. "You need a bigger knife."

I took a deep breath and shook my head. "I don't have one."

Morris turned toward the cliff. "Let's go."

So now, I was going fishing. It was just as well. I needed Morris's help if I were really going to stay out here in the woods. I'd watch my step, though, play along, see what I could learn.

"How far is the river?"

"Four, five mile maybe."

Morris led the way. We set off through the mostly bare trees along the foot of the limestone cliff and then across a steep hillside. Leaves rustled around our ankles, and I hopped over puddles in the deer tracks, trying to keep my sneakers at least sort of dry.

After more than an hour of hiking, we picked our way down a rocky path to reach the river. The sun hovered overhead. Noon. We had to eat sometime. The small river crept down a series of clear pools linked by whispering waterfalls.

"We are going to catch some minnows here. For bait." Morris produced a tiny net on a wire frame from his bag, and a soft bit of leather fell out. He picked it up and waved it at me. "You need a knife strap. Here." Morris tossed me the leather. "Made two with last year's deer hide. You can have this one."

"Thanks!"

Morris placed a finger across his mouth. "Shh. The fish, they hear talkin'."

———————◆●◆———————

A fish swished at the surface of the pool but didn't bite. Fishing wasn't producing lunch.

I scooted off the fallen tree, propped my fishing pole, and pulled my edible plants guide out of my back pocket. What could I find to eat? I flipped through the book. Summer plants, fall plants. Which?

I collected my gear and followed Morris as he led the way upstream, knelt, and pulled a bag of plastic netting labeled "onions" from the stream at his feet. It was stuffed with acorns, at least three pounds of them. "Supposed to be in running water for two days at least. These been there three days I think. Though I lose track of days sometimes."

"How do you keep track?"

He pulled a booklet from his bag. "Calendar. So, what date was it when you got here yesterday?"

I shrugged, acting nonchalant. "You tell me."

"October 18, 1969."

My knees gave way, and I sat down on a rock, hard and cold. "You sure?"

Fifty years from where I thought I was. Plus a few months.

I had to be able to explain this somehow.

It had started when I got into the green truck. The orange leaves. The short days. The antique cars—every single car on the road was one. The old-timey lettering on the billboards. The useless cell phone.

How could it be? My head buzzed like it held a hive of bees.

"Something wrong?" Morris took a step toward me, a puzzled expression on his face. "My calendar's off?"

"Uh, no. I don't think so."

He waited, standing there. "You okay?"

I took a deep breath, trying to not let him see my agitation. October 1969? No, it wasn't. It was June 2019.

It was summer. There shouldn't be acorns.

I placed my tingling forehead against my knee. I must be far, far from the reach of Aunt Trudy. But not in miles. Time. She wasn't even born yet. And neither were my parents.

Morris pulled a pencil stub from his pocket. "Let me show you how I use this. October eighteenth. A Saturday." He made a large X to cover the date, matching a row of X's on the previous days. "Whenever I go to Farmington to visit the food pantry at the Catholic church, I check the date. See if I lost count."

I tightened my shoelace and tried to keep my voice from wobbling. "You go there often?"

"Couple times a year. Just to get a can of coffee. Maybe a cookie. Listen in for a bit of news. I don't want nobody asking questions, so I ease on out of there and come back."

Standing next to the stream, I paged through my plants book, but my mind was elsewhere.

If there was a God, was this his idea of a joke?

I had no idea how to get back to 2019, even if I wanted to.

CHAPTER 9

Patience, persistence, and perspiration. I murmured Dad's words to myself as I waited for a rabbit to come within range.

I sucked in a breath as a rabbit sampled the air in the knee-high grass. Its ears swiveled.

I inched my gun upward to my cheek. The rabbit froze. I sighted on its head and fired. The rabbit flopped over.

I shot to my feet, punched the sky, and let out a whoop. Then I stopped myself.

I should go for two. After retrieving the carcass, I returned to my ready position. On the other side of the clearing, after a moment, a second rabbit sat on its haunches, its ears visible above the tall grass. I raised the gun. The rabbit darted to the side. I fired into its path, and it fell. Again, a kill.

I jumped high enough to touch a leaf in the tree overhead, joy lifting my feet. I did it. I could do it. I could make it living in these woods, thanks to Morris and my sharpshooter skills. I could live here a long time, no matter what century I was in. And I wouldn't have to eat acorns tonight. I could even invite Morris for dinner.

At my campsite, I started a fire and set my tin cooking pot filled with water on the portable grate. I threw sticks on the flames and piled more next to the impromptu fire ring. I rolled a good-sized rock next to the ring to use as place to sit. Then I rolled up another one.

I needed to figure out how to skin a rabbit and cut it up. I could ask Morris, but I didn't want to be in debt—any more than I already was.

I'd skinned and cut up a chicken once. I picked up the first rabbit carcass, started to work, and ended up with some chunks of meat. I did the second one. Then, like a good Boy Scout, I buried the parts I wasn't using so I wouldn't attract scavengers.

By the time darkness fell, a dusky aroma filled the air around the tent from the boiling pot. The fire spat and crackled. My mouth watered as I fed the fire.

A bobbing flashlight approached, along with a faint sound of footsteps swishing through leaves. Morris stepped into the firelight. "You got some rabbit?" A broad grin relaxed his face.

"I got two."

Morris nodded. "And got 'em all cleaned and skinned?"

"Did my best."

Morris laughed. "You'll be a woodsman yet."

I got out my Scout bowls and silverware, divided the stew into two portions, and we sat down to eat—and eat good.

"So, you from Shady Creek too?" I asked.

Morris turned the pot upside down on the grate. "Born there. My people are there."

"They still there?"

"I suppose so."

How was I going to say this? "I guess I don't know if I know them." I was fifty years away from that, after all.

"They mostly stay on the north side of the creek, and you people stay on the south side."

"I see black folks sometimes. Mostly at school." The races didn't mix, really. Probably things hadn't changed too much since 1969, I guessed.

Morris leaned forward, staring at the fire. "I got a cousin, Deon, maybe 'bout your age. And he got a sister, Sojo. One year younger. I think Deon tried Scouts once or twice." He stood and paced over to the big tree, then back. "My sweetheart Celia babysat for Deon and Sojo when they were little. That's how I got to know Celia."

"You got a sweetheart, Morris?"

"I did, three years ago. I suppose she done married somebody else now." His face crumpled, and he covered it with two hands for a moment. Then he dropped them and stared at the fire, a pinched look drawing lines of anxiety in his face.

"What happened?"

"I ain't talking about that." He turned quiet again. Then he stood, turned his back to me. "I'll show you how to fry a fish some time." Then he left.

I sat looking at the sky, thinking. What did I even know about the sixties anyway? A documentary I'd seen at school flashed pictures across my mind. Anti-war protests. Vietnam War. Hippies promoting peace. Assassinations.

A log shifted in the fire and sent sparks flying.

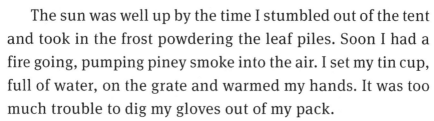

The sun was well up by the time I stumbled out of the tent and took in the frost powdering the leaf piles. Soon I had a fire going, pumping piney smoke into the air. I set my tin cup, full of water, on the grate and warmed my hands. It was too much trouble to dig my gloves out of my pack.

I headed to the field by the gravel road with my gun. Twenty minutes later, I returned with two more rabbits.

Morris stood by my campfire. He held his coffee cup and a tin plate containing fish he had fried, which he held out to me. "I think that aunt was wrong about you," he said.

I shook my head and knelt, laid the carcasses on a rock, and cut into one. "She's just mean. I don't know. Doesn't like young people around."

Morris picked up the fish, broke it in two, and handed me the bigger half. We stood there munching and then licked our fingers.

"You want to learn something else?" Morris put the empty tin plate upside-down next to the fire.

I stirred the stew pot. "Sure."

"We need to go down to the gravel road. I think we can leave that pot to boil for a minute. The critters, they won't go near the fire."

"Okay."

"We're going to look at Jerusalem artichokes."

"What's that?"

Morris led the way. "They grow near roads, in the hedge rows. A kind of sunflower."

"Do you eat them?" I trotted to catch up.

"Yep. The roots are like potatoes. You harvest them after frost when the plant has died back. Peel them, cook them. Good food for the winter."

"I wondered what you eat in the winter."

"I usually shoot me a deer and dry the meat, and I store up a lot of acorns and Jerusalem artichoke. Catch fish too. The rabbits, they get harder to find in winter. They're asleep or something."

"Ever got lonely after three years?"

Morris glanced sideways at me. "Nah. Not really."

I didn't believe him.

Why didn't he go back to Shady Creek?

We reached the gravel road and walked until we came to where dense shrubby growth stood next to it, probably untouched by a mower for many years. "This here's Jerusalem artichoke." Morris stepped into the brown dried brush.

The plants towered as tall as Morris. Leaves hung from the woody stems like faded brown flags.

I shook my head. "I hope I know what these are supposed to look like when they're growing."

"Little daisy flowers, yellow, high up on these long stalks."

Morris bent and wrestled with the bottom of a stem until a root ball came up in his hand. He turned it over and showed me. "See the little potatoes in the roots? Those are good to eat. And the longer you wait to harvest 'em, the bigger they get. They'll be bigger in a month."

A tiny breeze rustled leaves remaining on the trees. Winter was coming.

CHAPTER 10

I was getting the hang of this woodsman's life. A week of mostly sunny days flew by, X's marked on Morris's pocket calendar. Peace began to steal into my soul. No one was calling me stupid. I read, gathering information from the plant book. It really didn't matter what year I thought I was in.

Gradually, I relaxed. Morris simply gave me no reason to be afraid of him. He continued to show me things and divide his food with me. As I did with him. When you've shared hours of fishing with somebody, deep in the quiet woods, listening to the creak of the breeze in the branches and the trickling voice of the stream, it's hard to stay afraid. And I was coming to realize why my dad liked fishing. Fishermen just loved hanging out in the quiet. Catching fish was a bonus.

On a Sunday morning, I stood with Morris at the front of his cave, looking out at rain, munching on acorns, and whittling the peels off Jerusalem artichoke. I breathed deeply of the clean, cold, fresh scent of the rain.

"November, it rains for days and days. You just get used to it, and you go on about your life. All the other critters around here do." Morris's face was relaxed. The lines around his eyes hadn't returned for a while.

I made a face.

Morris chuckled. "Go on back to town, kid. You ought to be in school."

I flopped down onto the stool next to the fire. "You probably did better than me."

Morris remained standing, leaning against the cave wall, arms crossed. "I got through, and when I graduated, I got me a job in a landscaping business. Working on people's yards. I got drafted in sixty-five. Served in Vietnam for a year till I got hurt trying to save my buddy." A shadow crossed his face. "I don't even know what the war is all about, and I just 'bout died for it."

I frowned.

Morris collected his fishing bag and stick and raised them in a salute. "Man, I gotta get moving." He turned, backed into the downpour, and lowered himself down the cliff face.

I moved the coffeepot over the fire and threw in a log. Maybe I'd sip some coffee when it warmed up, even though I hated the bitter taste. Warm would be nice. I moved the artichoke bucket closer and sat down.

———◆●◆———

The rain quit thrumming on my tent in the night, and the sky was clear and light when I got up. Like I'd been doing every morning, I took a swig from my water bottle, picked up my gun, and hiked to the gravel road in the still frosty air. I sat on my stump at the edge of the field.

It was deer season for bow hunters, Morris had said, but I didn't see any hunters. I did see a doe pass like a phantom at the edge of the field. I was able to shoot two rabbits.

Back at the campsite, I stashed my gun in the tent. I cut up the rabbits quickly, put the meat and some water in my stew pot on the grate, and set about making a fire.

Morris appeared next to my tent, holding his coffee cup.

I shook my head. "How do you do that, move so quietly? There are leaves out there that you brush against."

Morris shrugged. "I've been practicing."

"I probably never even would have seen you out here."

"Somebody camped here last spring in this clearing for a week. And last fall, a bow hunter hung out in that tree for quite a while every morning." He nodded toward the large one at the side of my clearing. "Never knew I was here."

What would make him so determined not to be seen? I guessed Morris wasn't a criminal, but over time, I began to think maybe he used to be.

Morris said, "I'll tell you what it was like living in Shady Creek Colored Town."

"Sure, Morris."

"It's a close community. We all look after each other. But it ain't always peaceful. When I was a little kid, maybe eight years old, I got a brand-new kickball for a birthday present, and it went bouncing down the hill and across the street and into the creek." He took a sip from his cup.

"I was heading down the creek bank to pull it out of the rocks in the creek bed, you know, when these five white boys saw it and wanted it. I pulled it out and started back, but they must have decided it was theirs. Anyway, they beat me up. I had a black eye and a split lip, and no birthday present."

I stood there aghast. "How could they?"

He shrugged. "My momma told me if the white boys wanted my ball, I just should have let them have it. It ain't easy, dealing with folks who thinks they're better than you."

When had I thought I was better than the black kids in school who played endless basketball at recess? Or assumed black people must all be criminals?

Might as well put that right out there. "Being alone all the time must be better than prison."

"Prison?" Morris dropped the cup and scowled. "Who said anything about prison? You think I's avoiding—?" He turned toward me.

45

I backed up a step. "I don't know why else—"

Morris was shaking his head repeatedly, muttering. He jabbed a forefinger for emphasis. "I ain't never done nothing criminal, and don't you forget that."

"Well, what was it then? What are you doing here? You know why I'm here. Why are you out here?"

"I—"

Footsteps approached, rustling the leaves.

Morris lifted an eyebrow, laid his finger across his lips, and turned away, melting into the mottled shadows cast by the bare tree trunks.

A massive hunter in camouflage and orange cap swaggered into the clearing. He carried a huge white bow and quiver slung over his shoulder and wore an orange vest full of bulging pockets.

"Say you there! What you got? Cooking breakfast for me?"

I froze. The man's voice had a brassy ring to it.

"Hey. Hey! you're taking up my favorite clearing," he said. "I'm gonna be needing it."

"I'm leaving in a couple days."

"What do you mean, a couple days? Aren't you in school? You're playing hooky, ain't you?"

"I'm hunting. Shooting rabbits."

"You don't get it, Sonny Boy. This is my clearing. If your tent wasn't here, the deer'd be coming through. Up there's my deer blind." He indicated a broad limb in the oak Morris had pointed out, big enough to stand on, at a climbable height. "I've come to collect my deer from here. Today. So you got to clear out."

"But—"

With his free arm he shoved the stew pot into the fire. Then he kicked dirt into the flames. "Make way, boy. I'll give you one minute to take this tent down, or I'll do it for you." He raised a foot, aimed at a tent peg.

Where was Morris?

"Get that stuff out of this clearing. Now."

I pulled out the pegs, piled my belongings on top of the tent, rolled the whole thing up loosely, and dragged it through the bare trees as far as the limestone cliff. It was still within sight of the burly man in the orange and camo, so I dragged it farther, around a corner in the rock face. I used my shaking hands to shovel a leaf pile on top of it.

I headed back down the path.

"Now get yourself and whoever else is out here—get out of here." The man called from the clearing, loud and clear. There was no mistaking the menacing tone.

I took off running toward the main road, wishing Morris would show up. He was the only sane person I knew.

CHAPTER 11

When I reached the road, I leaned over, gasping for breath, my gut tied in a knot. I stayed bent over for several minutes as occasional vehicles buffeted me with gasoline fumes. I probably looked like I was puking. But I didn't care.

Farmington. I could find the food pantry, get a good meal, walk around town, and be back by the end of the day. No way that hunter would stay in the deer blind more than a few hours. Deer weren't active at midday.

Nothing coming. No cars. No green truck, no other vehicle.

A shiver crossed my shoulder blades.

I had to relax and get used to hitchhiking. There was no other way to get around.

But would Morris be there when I got back?

I wasn't ratting on him. I'd just go to the food pantry and head right back. Like a trip to the grocery store. What else did he want me to do?

How would I find my way back to this spot? My eyes sought a distinguishing mark. There it was. Not far ahead, the road cut through a hill, leaving white limestone rock walls on either side. I stood beside a stand of scrubby pine, unusual in the hardwood forest. Guess I knew something.

The road was quiet for so long I started walking. I heard a car approaching behind me, held out my thumb.

A rusty red pickup with rounded fenders pulled over, brakes screeching. A heap of scrap metal lay in the back, rattling. The driver was a middle-aged woman with straight blonde hair pulled back and tucked into a Cardinals baseball cap. "Where you going, kid?"

I moved over to speak into the open passenger-side window. "Farmington."

"That's where I'm heading." Her face creased into a half-smile. "Hop in."

I climbed into the cab. "Thanks for the ride."

She nodded and flipped the radio on.

"A Boy Named Sue"? What kind of music did these people listen to?

"So, what you up to?" she asked.

"I ..." What to say? "I was out looking for my dog." It wasn't a lie, really. I'd know my dog if I saw him. I just hadn't met him yet.

"Skipping school to find your dog?" She seemed amused.

"So far no luck," I said.

"We used to skip school to go swimming in the creek out back," she said. "Lost your dog ... you a rabbit hunter?"

"Yeah. Getting pretty good at it."

The faint aroma of barbecue potato chips mixed with the fresh woodsy air poured in through the windows. The load creaked and rattled like old bedsprings.

"My daddy's finally letting us clean up the back lot. Whole lot of junk metal, been there since I don't know how long. Maybe my grandad put it there."

I nodded.

"We just got used to looking at it." She tapped the steering wheel. "But my brother and me decided enough was enough. The homestead is going to look a whole lot better when it's gone."

"I bet the rabbits will like your place better now," I said.

"You bet."

Miles flew by, and the road signs started talking about Farmington.

"So," said the driver, "Where you want me to drop you?"

"The Catholic church."

She nodded. "Saint Joe's." She turned off the highway and onto a road that became a city street, then a bumpy main street. Older homes, a series of storefronts, and an imposing courthouse. Pedestrians wore business suits or tattered jeans, nothing odd there. But the hairstyles were something else. These people had way too much hair, men and women. It must weigh down their heads. Maybe I didn't look as unkempt as I thought.

When the driver let me out, the radio started "A Boy Named Sue" again—and she turned the radio off.

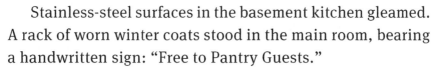

Stainless-steel surfaces in the basement kitchen gleamed. A rack of worn winter coats stood in the main room, bearing a handwritten sign: "Free to Pantry Guests."

I sat hunched over my turkey sandwich, mouth full. The mustard filled my senses in a way that it never had before, tangy and wild.

Did I have time to choose a coat for Morris? How about one for me?

"Eat up. You're skinnier than I ever was, young 'un." The heavy-set older black woman adjusted her apron and placed a glass of iced tea in front of me. "Good thing you got here when you did. We're closing for the day in five minutes."

I nodded.

"I bet you need some food to take along."

I swallowed. "A can of coffee." A gift for Morris. "And you got any Pop-Tarts? Maybe a loaf of bread? Coke Zero?"

"Coke Zero?"

Probably hadn't been invented yet. "Whatever you have."

"Coke."

"Fine."

"I'll get 'em." She strolled to a closed door marked "Food Pantry," opened it, and switched on the light. Shelves lined what looked like a large walk-in closet, full of canned goods and other supplies. She returned with a paper grocery bag, folded shut at the top, and laid it gently on the table beside me.

She wrinkled her nose, eyes twinkling. "No offense, young 'un, but you need a bath. You remind me of my son, after he's been working a long shift. Cookin', that's what he do. It's hot in that kitchen where he works."

"Oh, sorry. I'll get out of here in a second." I'd forgotten what the pungent effect of my presence might be like for others indoors.

"Now my other son, he's a soldier. Don't see too much of him these days." She nodded her head.

I had to say something, but I'd never met anyone before whose son was a soldier. What should I say? "You must be proud of him. Willing to make the supreme sacrifice and all."

"Yes, I am." She smiled really big as the clock hand moved one-minute past closing time.

I finished my lunch, snagged a brown down coat from the giveaway, and headed for the stairs holding the paper bag. "Bye. Thanks so much."

Time to head back to Morris. I walked past a few pedestrians as I entered the business district. An old lady wearing a skirt and white tennis shoes. A woman pushing a stroller. A man in a suit and hat, carrying a newspaper under his elbow.

Out here it didn't matter what I smelled like. They all ignored me.

Two girls in faded jeans and baggy men's shirts walked ahead of me on the sidewalk, hip-length hair swaying. Music poured from the open window of a nearby car—might be the Beach Boys. I wasn't really sure. All these rusted pickups, though. This was the country. Nobody was rich.

I left the courthouse square, heading for the highway on the main street.

A car door slammed across the street. A huge man got out of a white car with Illinois plates and glanced my way.

The bow hunter.

CHAPTER 12

"Hey, you there!" The bow hunter's words rang in my ears.

My hands trembled. I strode as fast as I could. I'd pretend to be deaf.

"Stop, thief! You broke into my car!"

Liar. His taunting tone hadn't changed.

A uniformed policeman leaned against a lamp post next to a shiny black-and-white police cruiser. Gray hair, flat-top haircut. Just what I didn't need. Someone asking questions I couldn't answer.

He glanced at the bow hunter, who was egging him on to chase me. What a jerk.

I ducked my head as I passed across the street from the cop.

I had to look like a guy in a hurry. Not running. I breathed deeply and willed my pounding heart to slow down.

Did I hear footsteps behind me?

"Hey, thief, still playing hooky?" The hooting call from the bow hunter a block behind me crashed into my ears.

"STOP!" A different voice, closer—a gravelly voice of command. The cop.

I didn't obey.

The heavy thrum-thrum of a large engine shook the air. A truck was coming up the road behind me. The vehicle might be heading out of town. I put out my thumb out.

Brakes whined, and sour diesel fumes brushed my nose. It was that green box truck. I must be on the same schedule as him, somehow. I squinted at the cab as it slowed beside me.

I glanced at the bow hunter, standing with hands on hips on a street corner, and, closer to me, the grim-faced policeman striding in my direction.

The Wizer's Pasta driver was grinning broadly, motioning to me to get in. Of course, he would have no idea that I was being followed by the cops.

I scrambled inside and leaned back in the seat, putting the grocery sack and the coat on the uncluttered front seat beside me.

The old guy shifted gears. His engine growled as we moved forward.

I drew a deep breath and let it out. From the radio came organ chords, majestic and warm, filling the cab.

Now I felt safe, hidden away from the world, shielded from dangers, a place of peace. And it smelled of cinnamon.

He was dressed differently today, in a navy-blue work uniform. On his sleeve some embroidered words made an arch: Wizer's Rescue. But his large brown eyes and close-cropped white hair remained the same.

I found my voice. "Thanks for picking me up."

"You're welcome." His head bobbed.

"And thanks for the food the other day."

This was my opportunity to ask questions. He had to know something about my strange predicament. "You picked me up in 2019 and set me down in 1969, didn't you?"

The old guy lifted a finger and cocked his head toward me, eyebrows raised. "That's a really strange thing to say. Now, why do you think that?"

"That day I saw you before, it was June in 2019 when I started the day, and when I got to that campsite it was October 1969. More than fifty years back. I was running away from

Aunt Trudy, but now she isn't even born yet. I've been stuck in 1969 ever since. I wish I knew why." The words tumbled out of my mouth, piling up in frustration.

He turned the wheel as we reached the highway with the air of an expert driver. "I see this situation is difficult for you. Well, I do know a bit about it, as it happens."

"And?" I leaned forward. He had to be an elf, or an angel, or something. Somebody like me who's time traveled can find himself believing in anything, just about.

"You made it to 1969 by yourself."

That was hard to believe. "How?"

"Cedar trees can be time gateways, I hear." He gestured with one hand. "Two together, maybe five feet apart. You step between any of those?"

"I'm in the woods. I don't know—"

"At about the time you did some time traveling?"

The roadside where I'd ducked away from a passing cop. Yes. I'd stepped between two young trees. Then the orange leaves had appeared everywhere. "I do remember that." I shifted in my seat. "Who are you? Or what are you?"

He lifted his eyebrows.

"You're a mage," I said. Well, he didn't actually look like a videogame mage, but anybody who knows about time traveling has to be special.

He smiled. "Oh, by the way, my name is Ned."

"I'm Richie."

"So, how's it going, Richie? I thought about you in all that wind and rain that night."

I nodded. "I had some trouble, but I'm doing fine. That is, I was until this morning. A hunter chased me away from my stuff."

"Lose any of it?"

"I don't know."

"You been out there about ten days?"

"Yeah."

"You miss your home?"

"No."

He scratched the stubble on his chin.

"You know a lot more about me than I know about you," I said. "Here's what I know about you. You know about time travel, and you're wearing something different today."

"I like to wear different uniforms," he said.

"Ah," I said.

"Let me tell you my haiku for the day," he said.

This one was about a whispering creek flowing through autumn leaves.

"Tell me about haiku," I said.

"Japanese poetry, five syllables in the first line, seven in the second line, five in the third line. Using word pictures about the seasons, usually."

"Why do you like it?"

He grinned, his smile lighting up his face. "It's likable, that's why."

The white limestone cliff beside the road came closer, and then the pine trees. I counted to ten to get a ways past the spot, keep it secret. "Can you let me out here?"

Clutching the paper bag and the down coat, I thanked the old man and hiked back up the road to the pine trees. There was no trace of the bow hunter's car, at least right now. So, he was still elsewhere. I found my things where I left them, under the pile of leaves at the foot of the cliff. When I climbed to the cave, though, except for a pile of firewood, there was no trace of Morris. He'd left. Only a hint of wood smoke lingered in the air. For the first time, I noticed how barren and cold the place was without a fire.

I shivered and put the bag of coffee down next to the fire ring. I kicked a stick of wood. The stick clattered as it fell from the pile, the sound echoing throughout the cave .

Did I dare stay here? Surely the bow hunter hadn't found the cave. Morris wouldn't have tipped him off, I was sure of it. Hadn't done it last year, wouldn't do it now.

I didn't want to hunt for another campsite, one that would have to be out in the open, colder and wetter. And, if I put my orange tent up somewhere else in the woods, any old hunter could bother me, just like the bow hunter had done.

At least for tonight, I'd see if I could stay hidden from the bow hunter. I moved what I had into the cave and climbed up where no one would find me.

Evenings were long. The cave echoed with my footsteps like a hollow tomb, and my voice grew gravelly from disuse. I even took to drinking the coffee I'd brought for Morris.

My own method of keeping track of the days involved making charcoal marks on the cave wall. Five, ten, thirteen days passed.

One night, I was frying fish in my iron frying pan. The wonderful smell tickled my nose and sent my belly rumbling. I hadn't eaten since breakfast.

Morris had helped me so much, showing me how to do all this. I missed him. Was I really going to stay out here hiding in this echoing rock all winter and beyond, with only myself to talk to?

It was going to get colder, a lot colder. Right now, frosty nights happened occasionally. In a month or two, it would be below freezing much or most of the time. It would snow now and then, and probably the snow wouldn't melt immediately.

I had a down coat now, but I was still wearing tennis shoes. Not boots.

Winter would be hard. I could look for one of these time gateways, two cedar trees five feet apart, escape to summer.

But if I entered it, who was to say what time I would land in? Why not 1919 instead of 2019?

Even though I hid every morning, maybe it was for no reason. I hadn't actually seen the bow hunter again. Maybe he'd found his kill after a few days, perched in the deer blind. Or maybe he hadn't and was still there in the mornings. I didn't know. But I didn't want to find out.

I pretended to be invisible, and maybe I was.

Then, one night, I heard scrabbling noises below the cave entrance. I held my breath.

CHAPTER 13

Someone was climbing up to the cave in the dark.

A tall man stood before me—his identity indistinct in the faint red light of the fire. I sucked in my breath, and my heart rate sped up.

"You gettin' along okay without me?"

Relief washed over me. Morris. "Man, am I glad to see you." The days flashed before my eyes. Going through the motions, finding food, collecting wood and water, but finding no joy in any of it. "It's been too long."

"Thought maybe you'd head back home. Go to school."

"I don't want to go to school." I sat on one of the logs. "So where you been?"

Morris sat on one, too, and waved an arm toward where the sun rose. "Over there. Couple miles, not too far." He grabbed my stick and stirred the fire.

I did not tell him sometimes I did want to go to school, when I stared into my evening campfire and chucked pinecones into it. I'd watch them sparkle and sizzle, smelling their piney smoke, feeling so lonely I could howl. Anyway, it was an impossibility.

"I was looking at my calendar, and I remembered I forgot to tell you something. Something you need to know."

"What's that?"

"November fifteenth through the twenty-fourth. Deer season. According to my calendar, the fifteenth is day after tomorrow. You need to be ready."

I exhaled. Hunters with guns roaming the woods. I hadn't even thought about it. "Thanks for telling me."

He nodded. "Time for me to shoot my own deer, too."

Maybe Morris would show me how. Show me what to do. How to prepare and dry the meat for the winter. How to keep all of that away from the critters.

He stirred the fire. "I was thinking I might want to come back."

I jumped to my feet and pumped the air. "Do it. Yes!"

He looked amused. "You still got that bow hunter hanging around here?"

"I think so. I don't go out in the early morning. He's gone by mid-morning."

He tossed his stick into the fire. "I could use some help pretty soon skinning my deer, cutting it up, that kind of thing. Maybe you'd like to know how to do it."

"Definitely."

Morris stood. Was he leaving?

"Stick around. My voice is getting all rusty." I poured hot water into two battered aluminum mugs and added bark. "Have some sassafras tea."

He sniffed it. "Tastes like medicine?"

"More like root beer. It's good for you, I think." I sipped mine.

"Not bad."

After a discussion of winter foraging strategies and some speculation on what might be happening in Shady Creek, Morris dumped out what remained of his tea. "Time to go back to my tent." He lowered himself down the cliff and, with a flicker of his flashlight, vanished.

I lay in my sleeping bag listening to the hoot of an owl in the distance. I drifted into dreamland, where I found myself on a gray day struggling through hip-deep snow, my sneaker-clad feet numb with cold, trying to climb a hill toward a cabin. Distant shots rang in my ears, and I crouched down. Was I the hunted one?

I turned to look. Right behind me was the bow hunter, this time with a gun, which he coolly aimed at me.

"No!" A sharp cry escaped my throat.

My voice woke me up. It was just a dream. The small patch of sky that I could see from my spot in the cave had turned a dark shade of gray. I sat up.

Was the real-life bow hunter out there? Had he heard me? I had to hope the answer to both of those was "no."

I waited to leave until close to noon, and then I walked toward the main road to look for more artichoke. The path wasn't even hidden anymore—grasses parted readily. The bow hunter had been using it twice a day, and I had occasionally used it too.

A police cruiser sat parked where the path met the road.

An officer sat at the steering wheel, and next to him was a large man in an orange vest. The bow hunter.

I crouched down behind a healthy set of bushes.

My mind raced. What were they doing there? Had my outcry in the early morning brought them?

Their footsteps rustled. "That kid," said a voice. "Reminds me of my little brother. Needs to get straightened out. Skipping school, and he had the moxie to take over my deer blind. Randy was always taking my stuff."

"He's not your brother, and he didn't know it was your deer blind," said the other voice, a raspy, gravelly voice. "Don't be too rough on him." That was the cop, surely.

"Well, he really took a wrong turn if he's been stealing cars."

"He's just a kid," said the gravelly voice. "His dad's worried sick about him. There's trouble in the family. Mom ran off to be a flower child in San Francisco, so she's got to be a druggie. That's hard on a kid. The dad will straighten him out when I bring him home." His voice sounded firm.

This car-thief kid had problems. And therefore, so did I, since the cop thought he was me. Worse, the cop seemed committed to the quest.

The footsteps faded back toward the cliff. I remained crouched for a while and then snuck off.

I spent most of the day at the river, gathering acorns and putting them out to soak. As the daylight began to fade, I walked the five miles back and stood in the clearing next to my old fire ring. If the cop had been here, he'd left no obvious trace. No posting nailed to a tree. No gum wrappers. It hadn't rained recently, so the ground here held no new footprints.

I climbed up the hill to the cliff where soil stayed damp. Traces of extra-large boots gouged the soil. Too big for Morris.

I followed the tracks to where they stopped and turned around. Did the intruders look up and find the cave? Hard to tell.

My heart thudded dully in my chest. I should move out. I should hike into the woods and set up my tent.

I brushed together a pile of dead leaves at the foot of the cliff to cover my tracks and then climbed up to the den. I had to decide what to do.

If I didn't wait here, I'd never find Morris again, but worse than that, the cave was compromised. He would come here looking for me and might even move in—only to be found.

But if I did wait here, the cop might find me.

Morris was my friend. I had to risk it. I'd stay at the cave until he showed up.

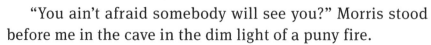

"You ain't afraid somebody will see you?" Morris stood before me in the cave in the dim light of a puny fire.

I hesitated. "Well, yes, I am. But I know who's looking for me, and I don't think he'll come at night."

Morris's belongings lay roped together at his feet.

"This morning a cop pulled over and parked at the path by the road," I said.

"Oh no." Morris was wearing all his clothes, a red lumberjack shirt over a jacket and tee shirt. "You think he found the cave?"

"I don't know for sure. There were two of them—the other was the bow hunter."

Morris sat down on a rock and rubbed his forehead.

"When I was in town, the bow hunter hollered 'Stop, thief' at me in front of the cop. Accused me of breaking into his car. So now the cop is after me. They were talking this morning, and I overheard. They think I'm some troubled kid who's a car thief."

"Humph. I don't call this fire laying low."

"I decided that cop isn't a woodsman. He won't be here at night."

"You being wise?" Morris stood. "It ain't safe here."

"I know."

Morris stopped. "Time to go back to the tent. For one winter I lived in my tent. You know what it's like living in a tent in hunting season?"

"No ..."

"Just stay inside the tent at dawn and dusk. That's what you do." Morris sat on a large rock next to the fire. "Unless we build a cabin."

"A cabin?"

"Sure. The settlers lived in cabins. There's two of us, we could build a log cabin," said Morris. "Can't stay here forever, I always knew that." He plucked his canteen from his pack and took a drink.

Morris would be better off if I had never come. Then he'd still have his cave.

He kicked at the fire.

"I'm tired. Hiked a long way lugging all this stuff, part of the way in pitch dark." He leaned back against the stony wall and closed his eyes.

I stared into the fire for a minute.

I pulled out my coffeepot, poured some water into it, and set it on the fire grate. "I'll make some tea."

We sat by the fire and sipped the tangy-smelling brew.

"You were about to tell me your story when the bow hunter interrupted," I said.

CHAPTER 14

"Why do I hide in the woods?" Morris stared into the fire. "'Cuz I expect they, somebody, is going to clap me in jail." The pinched look, gone for so long, returned. "They accused me of bothering a white woman—three years ago.

"I came back from the Vietnam War, got my wounded leg all healed up, and was getting ready to be married to my girl, Celia, working in the same landscaping business where my old dad had worked before he passed. Mowed lawns, raked leaves, planted trees, you name it, for white folks who live in the big houses there in Shady Creek.

"A particular old guy liked to talk to me, sometimes invited me up on the porch. That was Mr. Eldridge. Dad did his yard work for years. And when my dad passed, it was me working for Mr. Eldridge.

"Anyway, something he put in his shed, a silver teapot, turned up missing. His wife used to hide it out there in a bushel basket under some rags, to keep thieves from finding it. Can you believe that? She puts a silver teapot in a shed 'cause she thinks thieves would rob her house? I'd been in the shed plenty of times, but never looked twice at that bushel basket. The old guy come out of that house and confronted me. Thought for sure I did it. I told him, "I never took nothin' from you, Mr. Eldridge.""

"'You took it, Morris,' he says. Instead of bowing and scraping like my momma told me to, I hollered back. I says, 'I know nothing about this.'"

"I went on back home. Next thing you know, he's calling my mother, upsetting her."

"She says she's very sorry, I must have done it. I told her I had not done it. She says I might be able to keep the job if I give it back. I says, 'I never stole nothing.'"

"Now, Mr. Eldridge had a granddaughter, a pretty little thing, sixteen years old. But somebody scared her the next night, in the dark, as she was coming up on the porch. Tried to grab her or something. Not me. I know that. Maybe it was the person who took the teapot.

"The police started looking for me. They thought I must be the one who grabbed her.

"It was all a setup. Decades ago, the police accused my grandaddy of attacking a white girl, which he never would have done. They put him in jail, and then those townsfolk of Columbia, Missouri, came and pulled him out of there and hung him. Lynched him. No trial, no nothing." He paused. "I can't forget that date. April 29, 1923."

"My birthday," I breathed.

"My grandad never would have hurt a young girl. He was a good parent. They even figured out later he'd been at work at the time—two reliable people could testify. Not only that, somebody else in the jail told him *he'd* done it." Morris paused and clenched his hands. "I always wished I could go back in time and help my grandad. Save him. You know."

I paused. I was a time-traveler. Could I help him, save him? What an idea. "What did you do when the police accused you?" I asked.

"I kissed my Celia goodbye and hitchhiked out to the woods." His mouth turned down as he stared at his feet.

He threw a small log on the fire. It flared up. "And that is my story. I just want to live in peace."

I shook my head. Morris's life was so different from mine. Same town, Shady Creek. But it might as well be two different places.

I thought of all the times I'd seen black men on street corners in the city. People had told me they were dangerous, and I stayed away. If somebody had accused one of them of a crime, I would have assumed he did it.

What if all these men wanted was the same opportunities I had?

He'd told me his secret. I had one to tell too. "I got something to tell you, Morris."

"Yeah."

"My aunt won't come looking for me. She lives in the future. I did, too."

"What you mean?"

I tugged my plants book out of my pocket and found the back of the title page. "Published in 2019." I showed it to him.

"That don't make sense."

I lifted my water bottle and took a drink. "You ever saw a plastic bottle besides this one?"

"No. Never did."

I pulled out my cell phone, the flip kind. "This is my phone."

He opened it and lightly fingered the keys. "Where'd you get it?"

"It uses invisible waves. Like a radio. You touch the keys to dial a number. You send a message by typing words."

Morris lifted it to his ear. "It don't work.'"

I pushed the on-off button, but the phone didn't turn on. "The battery's dead."

"Fine, Richie." He yawned. "What you going to come up with next?"

"The phone. It needs a network to hook up to—it needs a grid. It needs a tower to bounce off. Maybe using satellites. For customer care phone calls. Like in India ..."

But Morris had crawled into his sleeping bag, and now I could hear faint snoring.

———————◆●◆———————

We set up camp in a clearing filled with huge boulders on the other side of the river and spent nine days laying low in the morning and evening. At midday, we gathered food and wood for smoking deer jerky. We found a deer track, full of night-time footprints. We occasionally saw or heard a hunter in the distance—none came very close, probably because of the rock pile. It was a good spot for snakes and not much else. Good thing the snakes were gone for the winter.

We gathered enough firewood to run three good-sized fires for three days, to smoke deer meat and keep the animals away. It was a big job for two people. How had Morris done it by himself?

Before dawn on the last day of deer season, the two of us waited for our prey, each of us sitting on a large oak branch. The deer track lay just a short distance away. Morris had his rifle across his lap. I didn't even bring my .22—that was for rabbits, not deer.

"Yes. Wind in our faces. That's what we need," he murmured. "So they don't smell us."

I stirred.

"You be quiet, now." His voice was barely a whisper, ten feet away.

"Okay," I breathed.

The hard part was staying still in the cold air. Somehow we both managed it, and the night sky draped with stars began to grow lighter.

A turkey gobbled not far away. Such a strange sound.

I heard rustling. Something was passing near us through the brush. Graceful silvery shapes, smaller than horses, blurry in the dark. Too blurry. Morris held his fire. Soon the deer were gone. It was still too dark.

The sky grew pale, and silent indistinct shapes passed like ghosts in the deer track. Too small. These must be coyotes, their tails hanging stiff behind them like bottle brushes.

The sky grew paler still.

More rustling. I could see three animals in single file, one with a rack of antlers.

Morris flicked the safety off with his thumb, lowered his head, and sighted along the gun.

His shot exploded in my eardrums. The buck dropped. A one-shot kill. The others bounded away as if leaping invisible fences.

"We got something to eat for Thanksgiving." Morris hung the carcass near our campsite, head-down to bleed out.

"When is Thanksgiving?"

"November twenty-seventh. Three days from now."

Aromas of turkey and stuffing, pumpkin pie and cranberry sauce wafted through my memory, and my mouth watered.

I pushed the idea away and started pacing to quiet my innards.

Morris shook his head. "I know it ain't like home. But maybe it's going to be more like the first Thanksgiving. I bet the pilgrims weren't eating any stuffing and gravy."

"Right." I started stacking sticks to make a fire. "*You* could go back home. See what Celia's up to, and your cousins."

He shook his head. "Ain't doing it."

"I bet the police aren't looking for you."

He grunted. "Too dangerous."

"Or I could go and find out." I'd risk tangling with the police myself. But if I could help Morris, maybe I should take the risk.

"Nah," he said.

I shrugged. "I could sneak out, find things out I think you'd want to know." I stood and walked through the knee-high boulders.

Maybe I should even try to time-travel back to save his grandfather. If I could figure out how. I owed a life-debt to Morris, after all. He'd saved me from dying of cold, and he'd risked revealing his hiding place to do it.

He stood too. "Going back to my folks? You don't know what you're talking about. It's dangerous out there. People get killed over nothing. And I only got one life to live."

From here, the world looked like a silvery, magical place. But really, it wasn't.

Morris knelt and chucked a stick into the fire. "They got Dr. King, didn't they?" His deep voice echoed with sadness.

Dr. King? Did he mean Martin Luther King? As in school holidays?

He went on, "Dr. King was marching. Marching just riles up those angry white folks. Remember the four little black girls who got killed by a firebomb while they were at Sunday school?"

"No."

"No lynching for me. You go to Shady Creek, and you ain't finding me here when you come back."

"Lynching doesn't happen anymore."

"What do you mean? Dr. King was shot dead by a white guy last year!" His voice cracked and broke.

CHAPTER 15

Rustling footsteps. A hunter strolled into our camp, bow casually carried on one shoulder. This guy was small and wiry, and his face wore a scowl. "You're stinking up the place." His low-pitched voice grated in my ears.

For two days, we'd kept guard against animals as the venison strips darkened and shriveled in the hickory-scented smoke from the fires. Morris put his coffee cup down and stood up, towering over the hunter. "Hunting season is over."

"Not bow season. You're running off any deer within two miles of here."

"This is my food for the winter."

"It's mine, too."

The hunter turned and pierced me with hazel eyes. "I've seen this kid somewhere before. What's this kid doing here?"

I had to act cool. "I have a lot of relatives around here."

He shook his head and considered my face. "Wooleyhans?"

"Yeah. Wooleyhans."

He stumped off into the boulder field, shooting off a comment, "I'll be back here tomorrow—you don't own the place."

Urgency grabbed me. "If he's seen me before, there must be a poster out there with my face on it. It has to be the car thief."

Morris frowned.

"That hunter will lead that cop right back here," I said. "I gotta go." I pulled a tent stake out of the ground and watched my orange tent fold inward.

Morris was folding his tent up too. "You go on ahead, get on your way." The pinched look had returned.

A hound bayed in the distance behind me. The sound sent a chill through my bones. I packed my belongings in thirty seconds, grabbed them, and started to run.

Maybe the dog wasn't looking for me. But maybe it was.

Walking in the river would throw off a dog. If I could stand the cold. I paused at the brink for only a few seconds.

The freezing water numbed my feet through the wet tennis shoes and made me slip and slide on the uneven stones as I stumbled down the stony river like it was a trail, the weight of my backpack throwing me off balance. It was a good thing I had a free hand to catch myself. I stumbled, barely keeping the .22 out of the water. Now I was wet to the knees.

Maybe I'd gone far enough. With the dog's distant voice echoing in my ears, I scrambled up the bank and threw myself behind one of those huge granite outcroppings that were everywhere in the Ozark woods. I couldn't go any further on numb feet and rough ground.

The dog's bay grew nearer.

What would the police do with me? They'd eventually figure out I wasn't the car thief. But I had no ID. I had no home.

I stripped off my shoes and socks and rubbed a foot vigorously with my knit hat. Too bad I didn't have spare shoes. But I did have spare socks. I dug them out of my pack, dried my feet with my spare sweatshirt, and put the socks on, the shoes, then the hat.

I mulled my few options as the dog's voice drew nearer. I stood up, jumped up and down, and started to feel a bit of my toes. But no, I had to hide. I crouched down and kept shifting my feet.

The dog's voice was close now. Down at the river. I made myself as small as I could. I heard splashing, and the baying stopped.

I held my breath. How well could the dog hear? My hiding place was probably only half a football field away from where the animal was. Was I downwind from him? Would he just flush me out?

There was nothing I could do but hunker down.

I heard a man. "He musta stepped into the river over here. Butch can't figure out where he went."

"He can't be too much ahead of us." The gravelly voice. Yes, the cop.

"Let's check the bank on this side for a bit, then the bank on the other side."

The voices and the rustling footsteps moved away. Going up the opposite side of the river. I could wait five minutes and slip away up the hill. But I didn't have long. They'd be right behind me as soon as they came back down my side of the water. I waited five minutes and scooted up the hill, bent over like a guerilla soldier. I needed to get to the road as fast as I could.

I topped the rise and ran. A vine rose out of nowhere and tripped me, sending me sprawling. After a stunned moment, I gathered my gun and my pack. I ran on, looking more carefully where I was going.

I could hear the traffic humming on the main road. Then not far behind me the singsong voice of the hound. He'd found my trail.

I ran again, heart pounding. Fear sent blood rushing through my ears. I crashed through the underbrush and made it to the road with the hound's bay still a ways back. I tossed the gun down out of sight and raised my thumb high, heading north.

Wouldn't anyone stop?

A shiny new red Chevy swept past me, a convertible with the top down, a white guy with sunglasses driving it.

I lifted my hand higher and faced the traffic, smiling hopefully.

A pickup truck rattled past.

The hound's voice drew nearer. And no cars were coming.

Let someone stop. I held my breath.

I heard grinding of gears before I saw it. Ned? No. A battered yellow truck appeared. It slowed and halted.

I grabbed my gun and vaulted into the cab. "Okay to bring my rabbit gun?"

"Sure." The driver nodded, a young black man with a military haircut and military boots.

We rumbled forward and picked up speed. The side mirror reflected two men—one a cop, the other a man in an orange hunting jacket with a tall red hound on a leash. They stood where I'd been five seconds ago, waving frantically at us to stop.

I pretended I didn't see them. But did the driver?

CHAPTER 16

I held my breath for a second, but I needed to distract him. "You going to war?"

He nodded gravely. "I am. We had a little furlough, a little time off, but now our unit is gathering in St. Louis. We're heading off to 'Nam." For a moment he gripped the steering wheel extra hard.

"Vietnam?" Is that what he meant?

"You're too young to get called up. But your time might come."

I'd never thought of that. Me, a soldier. "I suppose you're right." If I stayed stuck in 1969 till I was eighteen, that is.

"You live out in the country?" I asked. Most of the faces I saw on the road and in Farmington were white. But not all.

"I grew up in Farmington," he said. "My daddy was a cook, and my brother's a cook. Me, I want to see the world."

"Maybe I met your mother," I said. "At the food pantry in the Catholic Church."

A smile lit up his solemn face. "Yes, you sure did. How'd you know?"

"She said her son was a cook, and her other son was a soldier. She was proud of you. Also, there don't seem to be too many black people in Farmington."

"That's right, just a few of us. We have to stick together. Sometimes things are tough. People talking trash. And worse."

I sighed. His life was like Morris's in some ways.

The daylight faded as I stood in a neighborhood just north of downtown Shady Creek. Three rides over three hours had brought me here. I didn't think the cops would look for a white teen in the black section of town. And anyway, how would the cops in Farmington know to look for me in Shady Creek? I could have run all the way to Chicago for all they knew.

The town looked somewhat different from what I was used to fifty years in the future, but the layout of the streets was the same.

I shook my head, shouldered my pack, pulled my cap down, and started out. I had to find Morris's people.

What would I have felt months ago if a black teenager had come to my door? These folks were not going to welcome me.

But I had to find the house. I couldn't go back unless I did.

I held my .22 in my hand. I needed to ditch it somewhere. A strange white guy wandering around a black neighborhood with a rifle—I didn't need to be doing that.

I knelt and peered under the porch of a Baptist church. There was a spot I could leave the gun, and it would probably stay dry. I didn't know what else to do, so I shoved it in.

Cold darkness was falling. Now I had to find someone who knew Morris.

Tiny houses clung to the hillside close together, empty porches lit with bare bulbs. Occasional pedestrians passed me, going briskly somewhere. An old car rumbled by. I trudged up the hill, not knowing what else to do.

It would be awkward asking everybody I met whether they knew Morris. They'd all ask questions. Just the sort of situation Morris didn't want.

The name floated through my mind. Deon. Morris had said Deon was his cousin, about my age. I had to find Deon. If anybody was going to help me, he might.

I'd gone two blocks when four tall lanky guys maybe a little older than me materialized out of nowhere. They blocked the street, elbow to elbow, and their silhouettes loomed in the dim light from the front porches.

I edged to the side, hoping to squeeze past on the sidewalk.

They moved sideways with me. One of them sauntered forward, arms crossed, the threat now unmistakable. "What you doing here, white boy? You lost?"

My heart pounded hard, and I knew I needed to take a deep breath, but couldn't.

I searched their stony faces. They didn't want me here. I could see that.

I let my pack hang from one shoulder and showed the palms of my hands. "I'm just looking for a guy named Deon."

"What kind of business you got with Deon?"

"I got a message for him."

The tall one spoke first. "What's the message?"

"I just gotta' find Deon. It's private. From a relative."

The tall one grinned. He swaggered forward, reached out, and pulled my knit cap down over my eyes.

"You need to go back to your side of town."

I pulled the cap back up. The tall one's face was only inches from mine. Four against one, and every one of them bigger than me. My heart thundered in my ears.

One of them shoved my shoulder. I stepped back, eyes closed.

Another shove on the other shoulder. Another step back.

"You smell."

"I know."

"How come you don't take a bath?"

I opened my eyes. "I've been camping."

"Why'd you come here?"

"I got a message for him."

"Deon don't go camping."

"But I got a message for him."

"You going to go on your own? Or are we going to help you leave?"

"Please," I whispered. "I just need to talk to Deon."

They glanced at my big camping pack and then at each other before surrounding me on the sides and behind. "Let's go." They were forcing me ahead.

We approached a small brick house with a tiny concrete platform at the front door, one of a row of similar houses. In the dim light from the bare bulb in the porch ceiling, the tall guy rang the doorbell.

An older woman with gray hair drawn back into a bun came to the door. "What you boys want? Can't we even eat our supper in peace?"

The tall guy respectfully ducked his head. "'Scuse us, please. We want to speak to Deon. He there?"

"Sure he is." She stared at me for a minute. "I'll get him."

A tall, slender teen my age or so appeared, a comb stuck in his short Afro. He let the screen door fall shut behind him and faced me, eyebrows raised higher than the moon. "Who are you?"

"I gotta talk to you. Privately first. Please?" **Please** had worked wonders a minute ago. Maybe it would again.

I tugged on his elbow and led him over to the darkness of one side of the yard, leaving my escorts hanging out at the porch, sniffing the chocolate-chip aroma drifting through the open door.

"My name is Richie Roberts. I got news of your cousin Morris," I whispered.

"What?" he exclaimed.

"Morris. Your cousin," I continued in a soft voice.

He looked toward the street, then sized me up out of the corner of his eye.

I waited.

He scratched his head and pulled his plaid jacket closer around him. Finally he spoke, dropping his voice. "We could use news of Morris."

Whew.

He went on, "My grandma back there misses him something terrible. He's her nephew. And so does Celia."

His fiancée.

He stared at me, waiting, and I had to keep talking. "It's a secret that I'm here. The police might be looking for me. I haven't done anything actually wrong. Ran away to the woods. Not going to school. You keep my secret, I'll tell you about Morris."

CHAPTER 17

"Deal," he finally said. "I'll tell the boys to back off, and you can come in the house."

I nodded and followed him back to the porch.

"He's okay," Deon announced. "Thanks for bringing him over here. I'll take him inside."

The tall one sniffed the air. "You got any spare cookies?"

"Just a minute." Deon disappeared inside and came back with five cookies, one for each of us, which we gobbled up. Then he shooed them away, and I found myself in a tiny green living room overfilled with a green vinyl-covered sofa and coffee table, and beyond it a table and four chairs for eating.

The woman with the bun stood in the doorway to the kitchen, and a skinny teenage girl sat on one of the chairs at the table. She was maybe a little younger than me. Her hair was shaped into a stiff rounded cut, and she wore neat blue jeans and an orange turtleneck. The aroma of ham and chocolate-chip cookies was far stronger inside, sending my stomach growling. Deon introduced me to Miss Anna, his grandmother, and Sojo, his sister. "This is Richie," he said. "He knows Morris."

Suddenly, the warm indoor air felt stifling. I took my knit hat off and then realized my mistake when I saw Miss Anna's flared nostrils. "Uh, sorry." I clapped the hat back on. "I'll talk fast, and then I'll go back outside."

"Go on," Miss Anna said.

"Morris is living in the woods this side of Farmington. So am I. I ran into him in the middle of October."

My words riveted their attention.

"We've been hanging out together some, foraging. He's hiding because he's thinking the police in Shady Creek are out to get him. He wishes he could come back, but he won't do it 'cause he thinks he'll be thrown in jail and lynched."

Miss Anna drew in a deep breath, and a tear trickled down her cheek. Sojo crossed the little room and put her arm around Miss Anna's waist.

"He thinks his fiancée must have found somebody else by now. I decided to come here and find out the truth. So I could tell him."

"Let's sit down." Miss Anna dropped into a chair, and the rest of us followed suit. She brushed the tears away. "He's been out there hiding in the woods all this time? We thought he might be dead. Might have run off to somewhere far, far away. Gotten himself another identity or something."

"No. He's hiding because he's afraid."

"What's he afraid of?"

"The police."

"He got good reason to be afraid of the police?"

"Maybe not. At least, what he describes isn't a crime. Something to do with a missing silver teapot and a young white girl who thought somebody was attacking her. But it wasn't Morris. None of that was him."

Miss Anna shook her head. "He ain't never been charged with no crime. Ain't nobody out looking for him."

I launched out of the chair to stand up. "He said his granddaddy got lynched, and he thought he would be too."

84

Miss Anna rose. "That's true my father, his granddaddy, was lynched, but that was in 1923. More than forty years ago. Being in Vietnam changed Morris."

"Maybe so," I said.

Sojo's hands clasped Miss Anna's. Her eyes brightened. "Granny, maybe he'll come home."

Miss Anna turned to me. "Did he send you?"

"No, ma'am. I came on my own."

Sojo's mouth bowed into a smile. "Morris. We lost him. Maybe now we're going to find him."

"Celia?" I asked. "She married somebody else like he thinks?"

Sojo shook her head, eyes large. "No. She ain't even looking for nobody else. She's waiting for Morris." She bounced to her feet. "I gotta go tell her."

"Wait. Nobody can know I was here. Not until I leave, and then some."

"What you done?"

"Nothing but run away. Six weeks ago, I ran off to the woods, and I've been living there ..."

"So, you are hiding too." Miss Anna looked me directly in the eyes.

Morris's face flashed through my mind, its perpetual hunted expression on it. Was I like that?

She went on, "You can just tell him the police ain't looking for him, but Celia is, and he'd better get on home. And tell him I said so."

I nodded and stood. "That's what I needed to know." As I turned, my gut rumbled.

She pursed her lips. "Where you gonna go on a cold night like this?"

I shrugged.

"You had any supper?"

"No, ma'am."

She frowned. "Growing boy like you." She shot a glance at Deon, who stood behind me. "You made this agreement with him that we wouldn't tell anyone he was here?"

He nodded. "Yes, ma'am, I did."

"All right then. I'll abide by that. You too, right, Sojo?"

Sojo nodded.

Miss Anna crossed the room and laid a hand on my shoulder. "You can stay here, eat some supper here, and I'm inviting you to Thanksgiving at our house tomorrow. I'm cooking, and lots of people are coming over. We'll just say you are our friend Richie and leave it at that. They can wonder, they can ask, but we won't explain until you are long gone."

I nodded with a huge grin plastered on my face. "Thank you."

"First things first. You need a bath." She pointed down the tiny hallway on the other side of the archway to the kitchen. "Right down there, second door on the right."

I let the long-awaited warm shower spill across my head and shoulders and breathed in the sweet thick scent of shampoo. My thoughts wandered. Had the cop and the tracker with the dog taken down the license plate of the car I got into? Maybe they reached the soldier driver. That man knew I was headed to Shady Creek, even though he didn't take me all the way.

CHAPTER 18

Maybe I was a wild man now. But since I had the chance, I borrowed shorts and a tee shirt from Deon and threw all my clothes in the washer in the basement.

Before bedtime, we sat around the dining room table and talked. Miss Anna, it turned out, had a job sweeping and dusting at the local drugstore in downtown Shady Creek. For me in 2019, that storefront was a restaurant. But for her, the place was a drugstore that hadn't changed much since the 1920s—tin ceiling, plank floors, and all. Hard to keep clean. Sojo helped her sometimes after school. Deon too. Once there was a whites-only soda fountain, Deon said, and for some years now there had been no soda fountain.

"I didn't grow up around here," Miss Anna said. "In Chicago, and then in Columbia." A shadow of pain crossed her face. "Moved here to Shady Creek with my brother when I was about your age to live with our uncle."

She was an orphan too. It was her father who was lynched.

"Morris is your nephew," I said.

"Yes, my brother's son."

"Your brother is in Shady Creek?"

"He passed years ago."

I absorbed these details of their lives and tried to offer something in return. "My parents are dead. Killed in a car accident. I'm supposed to live with my aunt, over on the south side of Shady Creek. But I can't stand the mean things she says, and so I ran away."

Miss Anna nodded, the movement echoed by Deon and Sojo. They could tell I was speaking the truth.

I slept fitfully, wrapped in a sheet on the stiff vinyl sofa, feeling like an overcooked burrito in the warm air inside the little house. I'd have felt more comfortable in my tent outside.

I changed clothes, repacked my stuff, and stood my pack next to the back door. A quick exit might be in order. But the aromas of the feast made my stomach rumble all over again, advising me to stick around.

The doorbell rang at around 1:00 p.m., and soon eight or ten people crowded into the little house, sitting on the sofa, standing around the dining table, or cramming themselves into the kitchen.

I sat on an arm of the sofa, polishing the gravy off my plate with a dinner roll and feeling pleasantly stuffed, when the doorbell rang again. Maybe it was somebody bringing pie. It would be time for dessert soon.

"Celia!" A woman near the door hugged the newcomer, who sure enough carried a pie. "Come in!"

Celia! Was it Morris's Celia? My gaze turned to Deon. He stood at the door to the kitchen, plate balanced on one hand. He lifted his eyebrows at me for just a second, nodded, then looked back at the woman in the doorway. Yes, this was Morris's Celia.

She pulled off her coat, which got passed hand-over-hand all the way back to the hallway and presumably a bedroom. She was a slim, shapely woman, hair styled smooth and shoulder-length. She greeted those near her with hugs and kisses.

Her gaze locked with mine, and her eyebrow shot up. My cue. I put the plate down on the coffee table and squeezed toward her in the crowd. "Mighty glad to meet you. My name's Richie. Friend of Deon's." I shook her hand. Same as with everybody else.

Her eyebrows drew down, and then smoothed out. "Glad to meet you too, Richie. Any friend of Deon's is a friend of mine."

"Thank you," I said. Then I started to back away.

"You look familiar." She tilted her head, as if to examine me.

Oh, no, was there a poster with my face on it in this town too? My hands gripped my forearms, knuckles white. "I, uh, haven't met you before." I looked around for help from Deon, but he was not to be seen, at least from where I stood near the front door. "Maybe I look like somebody you know."

She nodded slowly. "Yes, that must be it." But the question in her eyes remained.

Maybe I should pull her aside and tell her about Morris. No. Too risky.

But I'd come here to find her. Yes. I'd take the risk.

I stepped toward her. "Could I ask you a question? In private? Out on the porch?"

She hung back.

I turned and touched her elbow. "Please." I dropped my voice. "It's about Morris."

She clapped a hand over her mouth, and a shriek escaped her fingers.

"Shh." I laid a finger across my lips and glanced around. Had anyone heard?

The screen door behind me squeaked, and the doorbell rang.

I turned to look.

It was a red-haired guy my age. Another white guy in this gathering. Beside him, someone who must be his father carried a pie. What were they doing here?

The kid glanced at me. "Pete!" he cried out, good and loud. "Pete, what are you doing here? The cops are looking for you. Heard you were stealing cars." Then he squinted at me. "Pete?"

"My name is Richie," I said. So that's who my look-alike was. Some guy from Shady Creek named Pete.

I stepped out the door toward the red-haired guy and paused right next to him, in the only space left on the tiny porch. "Shh," I muttered. "I don't know who Pete is, but I sure wish you hadn't said that. Please just talk to Deon."

He looked me carefully in the face under the light. "You aren't Pete Hungerford."

"No," I said.

As the voices in the room behind me grew louder, I scrambled around the house to the back door, grabbed my pack, and took off down the street running.

A siren wailed in the distance. Was it coming this way? I looked around for an open garage to hide in. But none of the little houses seemed to have any.

The siren grew closer. What else could I do? I ran down the hill toward the church where I'd left my gun.

The squad car turned onto the road at the bottom of the hill just as I got there. I made myself walk slowly on rubbery knees, pretending it was perfectly normal for me to be sauntering down this particular road on Thanksgiving, wearing a camping backpack piled high with tent and sleeping bag. I pulled my knit hat down over my curls as far as it would go.

I was no longer in the black neighborhood, but on the border. I definitely looked out of place because of the backpack, but not so much because of my race.

The officer slowed the car to a crawl as it passed me. I pulled my head up and nodded at him. A young man, he was eyeballing me like crazy.

Were they looking for a kid guy named Pete in Shady Creek this night, or just for a disturbance? I held my breath, and my insides felt like a washing machine churning a full load.

Lights flashing, he kept going and turned up the street to Deon's house.

I bolted for the church at the foot of the hill and grabbed my gun from its hiding place. But where could I go?

The creek. I stumbled over rough turf and then eased my body down the embankment. I hunkered down and knelt on a cold stone, backpack in my arms. I could hear the trickle of water near my feet.

Tires crunched in the parking lot above. Flashing red lights pierced the gray sky. My heartbeat thundered in my ears as I crouched gripping the backpack "Go away. Please," I whispered.

CHAPTER 19

Tires spun in gravel as the squad car left. My hands relaxed. The purr of the engine faded.

I took four different rides to my old drop-off spot near the cave. It was growing dark when a creaky Buick sedan let me out, and its ancient driver waved goodbye.

Dry leaves littered the forest floor, and bare branches grasped at the sky. A shiver shook my body, and I pulled my hat down low over my ears. Tennis shoes weren't a good match for cold weather.

At the foot of the cliff below the cave, I squatted and ran my hand over the damp ground. No signs that someone had been there since the last rain.

I'd been gone one night, long enough for Morris to set up camp somewhere and leave me a message at the cave. A cryptic message that no one else could understand. He'd know I wouldn't be in town long.

He must have come and gone like a cat, leaving no traces.

I grabbed a handhold and started to pull myself up. With my news, he'd go back to Shady Creek now. He had no reason not to. He'd go back, leaving me eating the deer jerky and looking for ways to keep warm. I could handle it. I chose to be here.

I couldn't wait to see him to deliver the good news. My heartbeat quickened as I pulled myself up to the mouth of the den.

The cave was lit by afternoon sunlight. No campfire had burned there for at least a couple of weeks, but our old stack of firewood remained, along with my charcoal marks counting the days. I crouched and looked carefully for the clue. I crawled around and felt in the dark places with my hands.

But I found no tin can. I could find no evidence of a message from Morris at all, stuck in a tin can or otherwise. I swallowed hard when I realized it, dropped to the ground, and let my chin sag against my hands. My gut felt like I'd swallowed a boulder.

I had to risk staying there for a short time. I had no other way to reach Morris. After a few moments I lit a fire, laid out my bedroll, and drowsed with an empty stomach as the daylight faded.

I relaxed in the velvet silence of the winter woods and ran my thumb over the soft deerskin knife sheath Morris had given me. Would I find him? I shivered.

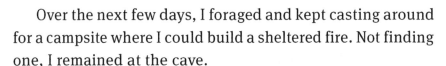

Over the next few days, I foraged and kept casting around for a campsite where I could build a sheltered fire. Not finding one, I remained at the cave.

But every day I stayed made it more likely that the Farmington cop with the gravelly voice would find me, haul me in for questioning, and never let me come back.

Morris would never get the message that he could come home.

Questions swirled in my mind. What if I time-traveled again? What if I went to 1923? Could I help Morris that way? What if Morris' granddaddy hadn't been lynched? Would Morris stop hiding in the woods? Yes, I'd do it. If I could figure out how.

The next day dawned clear and well above freezing—so warm I wore my jacket instead of my coat.

It was the perfect weather for my police friend to come and check on the cave.

I didn't know where I was going, but I packed up. I did my best to leave the cave looking as it had when I got there, like no one had been around for a long time. I packed up my acorns and Jerusalem artichoke and climbed down the cliff, clutching my .22.

The fumes of passing cars stank up the air as I walked along the highway. I asked for a ride north, hand raised, thumb out.

A police car from Farmington flew by, heading somewhere. I ducked my head and hoped he hadn't seen me.

Then I could hear him slow down, pull over, and turn around.

Oh, no. It was him, and he'd recognized me.

What could I do?

He'd catch me for sure. And I didn't have any way to prove who I really was.

Morris would never hear the good news.

Morris. Maybe it was time to try to time-travel to 1923.

I dropped my gear in the weeds beside the road and raced away into the woods. I spotted two cedar trees, slender and young, not far apart. A gateway. Past or future, I didn't know.

I plunged through it. Ned's face flashed across my field of vision as everything around me turned to gray.

CHAPTER 20

I staggered with nausea and disorientation, blinking, and taking deep breaths. An old car horn beeped. Something shoved me from behind, and all went black.

I opened my eyes and found myself lying on a cot in a rather large room. A heavy sweet smell teased my nose, and my head felt like it was going to split open.

Where was I?

As I stirred, an older white woman in a baggy dress and white apron walked toward me. A few strands of gray stood out in her dark hair, pulled back into a bun. "It's about time you came to, son," she said, leaning forward. "You've been out since yesterday." She gently touched my forehead and gave me a soft smile.

I struggled to sit up, making the headache worse. "Oww," I said, and lay back down.

I slowly took in my surroundings. A mammoth black woodstove radiated heat at one end of the room. Near the window stood a simple table with two chairs. A wooden box hung on the wall. I recognized it from the movies—it was a very early telephone, with a piece held to the ear by a cord and a separate mouthpiece to talk into. The room had few furnishings.

I'd gone back in time again, all right.

I touched the goose-egg on the side of my head and lifted my head, trying to sit up again.

"You don't need to sit up yet, dear," said the woman. "I'm Mrs. McLaren. What's your name?" She spoke with a bit of a drawl.

"Richie. Richie Roberts," I mumbled.

When I woke up again, my stomach was growling as a delicious smell wafted from the oven. Mrs. McLaren put down her knitting at the kitchen table and came over to my bedside. "You feel any better, Richie? You've been asleep for two days now. It's Friday afternoon." Her soft hand brushed the curls out of my eyes. My mom had done that whenever I was sick, and Aunt Trudy never had. A pang shot through me. I closed my eyes for a brief minute.

This woman must be a mom too.

I sat up and gingerly felt my head. The swelling had gone down, and the headache was nearly gone! I swung my feet to the floor and sat there. "I feel pretty good," I said.

"My husband was driving his car down Broadway, and wouldn't you know it, you appeared out of nowhere standing in the street right in front of him. It was the darndest thing, he said. He couldn't stop. So he hit you. Couldn't figure out where you came from."

"Yeah, I'll bet," I muttered.

She was clearly waiting for me to explain, but I couldn't.

I had to figure out where I was, and what year I was in, without looking obviously clueless.

If he hit me on Broadway, that meant I'd landed in a town or a city. But I'd started in the woods. So this time travel thing involved moving not just in time, but in space too.

Mrs. McLaren fed me chicken and some apple cobbler, and I lay down again, feeling dizzy. It must have been the next day when I awoke feeling good and ate some breakfast. She sent me out past the living room to the front porch to talk to Mr. McLaren.

Tulips waved from the flower bed, and birds made a huge racket in the trees. In my strange journey, I'd started in summer, gone to fall, and now it was spring.

Gray-haired Mr. McLaren sat at a table on the front porch, papers filled with numbers spread out in front of him, his narrow-brimmed hat perched on the back of his head. As I approached, he lifted wire-rimmed glasses from his nose.

"I sure didn't see you coming. So, my car hit you. There you were, knocked out on the side of the road, and nobody nearby had ever seen you before."

"I'm from St. Louis."

"Richie, how'd you get here?"

I thought fast. Clearly, I was decades before 1969. "My uncle and I have been hopping freight trains." I'd seen a documentary about hobos in the Great Depression doing the equivalent of hitchhiking, but on freight trains. And Morris wasn't my uncle, but I'd claim him anyway. "We got off here, and now I don't know where he is."

Mr. McLaren shook his head. "We didn't see any other strangers at the scene. I carried you home, not wanting to leave you lying there."

A black car with froglike headlamps came down the street at a slow pace and turned into the driveway of the building next door—a wide white building. Mr. McLaren stood and went down the porch steps.

I lingered, and my glance fell on the newspaper next to his chair. "*Columbia Evening Missourian*," stood out in big words at the top of the page. Under that, the name of the town—Columbia, Missouri. And the date: Friday, April 23, 1923.

I'd landed nearly 100 years from my own time. And my birthday was just a week away.

My birthday in 1923—that was the day Morris's grandad had been lynched. In Columbia.

Indeed, somehow I had landed at the right time. I could do something about it. Make a real difference in Morris's life, not to mention his grandfather's. My being here was Ned's doing, I was sure of that.

But I only had a week.

First, I had to figure some things out, like how I was going to feed myself. I couldn't expect the McLaren's to take in a pet fourteen-year-old and keep feeding me. There was no way I could forage in a town like this. I needed a job. I sat down on the front steps and watched Mr. McLaren. Now I could see the sign in front of the white building: McLaren's Auto Garage.

A man got out. His shiny black car was a beauty. Ford Model T, the real deal.

I wanted to see the car, but even more, I wanted to find out more about where I was. "I'm going to take a little walk down the block," I called to Mr. McLaren.

"You had quite a knock on the head," he said. "Be careful."

I started down the sidewalk and dodged a couple of chickens that seemed to be looking for something they lost. The neighborhood was nice, with a few businesses scattered through it, including a little grocery store across the street.

I came to a stack of newspapers bound in string, sitting on a street corner. A clatter of footsteps on the pavement behind me made me turn around. Three guys about my age flew toward me, one of them throwing something at the other two. Grass?

The skinny one with glasses pointed to my jeans. "You work on a farm or something? You got waist overalls on." In contrast, they wore knee-length pants and long socks.

Waist overalls? "Haven't done that," I said. "But I need a job."

The short one pulled out a small knife and cut the string on a bundle of newspapers. Then they each grabbed an armful from the stack and turned to leave.

"You got any ideas?" I asked.

Shorty shook his head.

The chubby one looked at my waist overalls. "Why don't you find a farm? There's some not too far away, edge of town. They got cows to milk." Then they charged down the street.

Mr. McLaren stood talking to the Model T driver when I returned, a man with massive shoulders. A splash of mud marred one of his boots and one leg of the jeans. Maybe he was a farmer. Maybe he needed a hired hand.

A tall, stooped man in overalls lifted the hood. The three of them conferred.

Nobody was paying any attention to me, so I made my way to a place where I could see. The engine was positioned in its space with plenty of room around it, unlike inside the cars I knew.

"Well," drawled Mr. McLaren. "You never seen a car under the hood before?"

"Not one like this." I grinned.

He nodded. "Well, take a look."

The tall, stooped man, Silas, went to get the battery tester. Ultimately, he pronounced the battery to be faulty, and he went to get a replacement. It didn't take long. "One dollar fifty cents," Mr. McLaren announced.

The customer dug in his pocket for his wallet and handed over some coins and a large greenback. The bills were a bit bigger than what I was used to. Money apparently wasn't that different in 1923, except being worth a lot more.

Of course, I didn't have any.

"Sir," I asked the Model T man, "You have anything I could do for you? I'm looking for a job."

He shook his head. "Not right now, son. I got all the help I need. You could check back in a couple weeks."

I let out the breath I didn't realize I'd been holding. "Thanks," I said. I couldn't keep the hollow sound of disappointment out of my voice.

Silas put his tools away on a shelf, and then he slouched out of the garage and approached Mr. McLaren. "Where'd you find him?" he asked, looking at me with suspicion.

"Just about ran over him the other day. Now he's feeling better. Guess he's another one of those youngsters who just have to see what these automobiles are all about."

The evening air was getting cooler, so I wrapped my jacket closer. Mr. McLaren pulled out a plain silver pocket watch and consulted it. He glanced at me, clearly thinking. "Tell you what. I'll let you stay here a few days, in the garage, eat in the kitchen. We'll see if you can make yourself useful enough around the house and in the shop to justify your keep. Silas, show him around, please."

"Thank you, sir," I said to Mr. McLaren.

Silas motioned for me to follow. "You call me Mr. Wilson," he said.

CHAPTER 21

We walked through the shop, where the greasy odor of motor oil hung heavy in the air. Parts and tools filled disorderly shelves along the walls.

Behind a closed door at the back of the shop was a long, narrow room the width of the garage, with a cot and a simple table and chairs. Another door seemed to lead to the outside.

"You'll be sleeping here," Silas said gruffly. "It was my bed until about a month ago. I got my own place now. Ain't just yours, though. The help eat lunch in here. Mr. McLaren, from time to time he sits at that table and works on the books." He shook his head. "What he wants with a Communist long-hair like you, I don't know."

"I'd like to get my hair cut," I said, trying to be friendly.

"Go down to the barbershop on the square, then," said Silas. "Five cent."

He turned to leave the way we had come. "Well, see you on Monday. If Mrs. McLaren keeps feeding you."

He lowered the garage door behind him, and with a click it locked.

The room contained a chipped, dirty mirror hung on the wall over a simple sink with one faucet—cold water only. My reflection did look pretty different from these people with my hatless cloud of black curls. Communist?

In the dim light from the bare bulb on the wall, I tried a smaller door and found it led to a toilet. I checked the cot. In April, the thin blanket would do. I had a pillow and a sheet, too. It was better shelter than my tent, all in all.

I sighed and flopped down to sit on the cot for a minute, and then I headed back next door.

Mrs. McLaren thought I needed a haircut, too, and soon offered me turnips and ham. She also wanted to know more about riding freight trains, probing me with gentle questions.

"What are you going to do without your uncle?" She sat down across from me at the kitchen table.

I swallowed and shrugged. "I really don't know. Hope he finds me, I guess."

She picked up her knitting. "Maybe he'll come looking for you if you stay here a few more days."

A quaint black-and-white photo on the wall, lit by a simple light fixture next to it, caught my attention. It was a portrait of a young man with short curly dark hair and jaunty cap, wearing an oddly cut jacket and tie.

"Who's that?" I asked.

Her face grew sad. "That's our son, our only child, Frederick. He was killed in the Great War."

Great War? Uncertainty clamped my midsection. "I'm really sorry to hear that, ma'am," I said.

She took a deep breath. "You look a bit like him, really."

I blinked. "I'm sorry."

"No, no, no. I like to be reminded of him. It helps me remember."

"How old was he when he died?"

"Eighteen."

"I'm fourteen."

"At your age, he loved to help his dad in the car shop." She glanced at my hair. "I used to cut his curly hair. A lot like yours."

"If you want to cut mine, you could. I don't have money to pay a barber."

Standing up, she wiped a tear from the corner of her eye and moved to the sink to rearrange the dishes stacked there.

After I finished eating, she put a chair on the back stoop and cut my hair, dropping plenty of curls. Then she found a cap for me—like the ones the newsboys wore. She plopped it on my head. "It was Frederick's," she said.

"Thank you," I said.

"Richie, I do need some help with chores around here. We had to let Bessie go this week, so we're without laundry help. And then there's the lawn mowing. Mr. McLaren hasn't had time to do it, and he's getting a bit lame anyway."

"Yes, ma'am. I'd be glad to help."

"Mr. McLaren said you could start work at the shop tomorrow after lunch. He'll have time to show you some things then. We'll work on laundry on Monday."

That meant I had to use tomorrow morning, Saturday morning, to find Morris's grandfather.

"Thank you again, Mrs. McLaren."

I trotted down the back steps toward the garage. If only I could look up the Great War and some facts about cars in 1923. Not to mention lawn mowers and all the men named Scott in Columbia, Missouri. Didn't anyone have the sense to invent a database?

Morris's grandfather only had a week to live. I had to find him.

CHAPTER 22

Saturday, after scrambled eggs, I headed out to look for Morris's grandfather. For starters, I'd look for a black neighborhood.

I struck out toward the rising sun. I walked fast. I had to find him. Soon.

Houses began getting smaller as I walked. But it was clearly a white neighborhood. At the edge of town, I turned right and kept going.

Soon I found Mizzou. In fact, the University of Missouri was where my father had wanted me to go. I found a large, attractive quadrangle of red brick buildings with white trim and another group of white buildings.

A few students lounged around, dressed in what looked like uncomfortably formal clothing—dress pants and shirts for the guys, dresses for the girls, all wearing hats. All were white.

Because of my jeans, I stuck out in the crowd, but I kept walking and hoped nobody would notice me. Out of the corner of my eye, I saw someone behind me in the distance. Then he vanished. A shiver passed between my shoulder blades.

I stood at the brink of a wide ravine filled with brush. At the bottom twined a railroad track and a stream. I slipped and slid down the slope and started walking along the railroad track. I heard rumbling in the distance, the rails trembling as the noise got louder and nearer.

A huge black engine chuffed past me, casting pungent white smoke and little bits of black ash everywhere. It pulled an open car full of coal and eight box cars behind it, cars that didn't look that different from the ones a hundred years in the future. The engineer nodded at me, and I nodded back.

So, that was how I supposedly got here. In one of those freight cars. I was glad to see one, at least, had a door open, and such a trip would actually be possible.

I heard rustling behind me. Someone was following me, for real. I picked up my pace and ran along the tracks, beneath a bridge carrying a road thirty feet above me across the ravine.

Past a small train station, the track ended. The stream smelled bad, like a sewer. When I got to some wood shacks, I slowed to a walk. The unpainted cabins backed up to the stream, with a little wood building behind each.

Several black people hung out on each wood-floored porch, sometimes more. As soon as I showed up, though, they'd vanish inside.

Chickens clucked and scratched the dirt. Three children stood on a rock next to the putrid water, glanced at me, and then scampered into the nearest shack. An unseen hand flicked a curtain at a dirty window.

Looking around, once again I caught movement behind me out of the corner of my eye. I froze and waited.

A middle-aged woman came out of one of the shacks, fanned herself with her hand, and lifted a gray metal bucket before she headed down some steps to a water pump. A well, surely. A well reaching down to contaminated water. While she walked, she glanced over at me. "What's the matter, young-un? You ain't never seen this part of town?"

"No, ma'am."

"Most white folks never comes over here. You got business?" she asked conversationally as she bent over to place the bucket under the pump and started moving the big lever up and down, one hand on her back. Water trickled out.

"I'm looking for someone," I said.

"Who's that?"

"A Mr. Scott."

"Oh," she said, waving her hand vaguely off toward the east, "Mr. James Scott lives over that way."

"Here, let me do that for you."

She looked at me with amazement and stepped back. "Be my guest."

I easily filled the bucket.

She covered her mouth. Was she hiding a smile? I grabbed the handle and struggled to carry it up to the porch without spilling it. "There you go."

Then I retreated to the yard. She was indeed smiling now. "Thank you, young un. You done blessed my heart and my bad back today."

"You're welcome," I said.

"Mr. Scott, he's a big man in the colored community. Led our parade last year."

Her eyes turned to something behind me. I turned around and saw Silas Wilson, ten feet away. He stared at me with squinted eyes. "What do you think you're doing?" he asked.

"Just leaving," I said.

We walked past more shacks, which gave way to small but more normal houses on dirt streets, with occasional black people visible. The houses got bigger and bigger as we got farther from the creek, but the streets were still dirt, and the creek still stank.

A hip-hop song flowed through my mind, and I hummed along with it. In the silence, I even sang a couple of lines:

"I'm a rebel in the night." Until Silas turned to me and raised his eyebrows. "What's that you're singing, boy?"

"Uh, nothing."

Silas and I crossed into the brick-paved white business district, headed back toward McLaren's. As soon as we were out of the black neighborhood, he turned and faced me.

"Where'd you say you were from?" he asked.

"St. Louis," I said.

"Don't give me that baloney. They don't do things that different in St. Louis. I lived there when I was a kid, and I know. I think you ain't from St. Louis. Or else you are just plain ignorant." He stared at me. "We got rules in this town," he hissed. "And helping that woman, you just broke 'em. We got to keep these people in their place."

I had to get away from this guy. "Excuse me. I'm on my way to church," I said. I turned left down a street where a large white stone church stood on the corner. Would it be open on a Saturday morning?

I slipped inside the building, empty except for rows of pews, but filled with organ chords that set my skull to vibrating. I let out a big breath. Silas hadn't followed.

After a minute, I focused on the music. It reminded me of tunes I'd heard on the radio in the Wizer's Pasta truck. Rich and peaceful. I settled down to listen to the organist practice, eyes closed.

A minute later, the door creaked open and someone came in. Footsteps approached on the hardwood floor, and someone sat next to me. Silas? I opened my eyes.

It was Ned, wearing the same sort of clothes as Mr. McLaren—khaki pants, white shirt, tie that only came three-quarters of the way down his front, and a narrow-brimmed hat, which he held in his hand. He looked pretty different, like he actually belonged in the 1920s.

He clapped me on the shoulder with a big warm hand. "Keep up the good work, Richie."

Then he was gone.

I shook my head. Was he real, or was I dreaming him?

No truck this time. But then, his truck wasn't as old as the vehicles I saw around me in 1923. He couldn't drive it here. He had to have some other way to get around. But actually, he didn't seem to need one. He just popped up, and then he vanished.

My friend Ethan had had an imaginary friend when he was four years old. So, it sure looked to me like I had a mage/angel/elf friend, same deal.

But I was fourteen, not four. And Ned wasn't imaginary. He'd given me a ride, twice.

My life was too puzzling. Well, I'd go with the flow. Think about creeks flowing through autumn leaves. Listen to the majestic music. Rest.

After ten more minutes soaking up the peace in the sanctuary, I snuck out. I didn't see Silas outside.

CHAPTER 23

Having lost Silas, I headed back toward the black neighborhood. I had to be closing in on Mr. Scott.

I just didn't know what to tell him. I'd been pretty good at making up stories on the spot, about my lost uncle and hopping trains. I'd just make up something, I guessed. I'd aim for telling him the truth—he had to be careful.

I turned off Broadway, lined with one- or two-story brick storefronts, onto Third Street. As I did so, I left the brick-paved white-only part of town for dirt-covered streets. The stench of the creek filled my nose, and I heard it gurgling next to the road. I wondered once again why they didn't do something about cleaning it up, not the least for the people who used wells next to it. It was a setup for disease—I remembered that from my Scout manual.

Medium-sized houses crowded the streets here, a number of blocks from the wretched settlement of shacks on the downstream banks of the creek. People were out walking, maybe going somewhere, maybe not. I was the only white person I could see.

How many black people felt nervous, moving around in the white community? Now it was my turn. That's what I told myself.

Nearly everyone avoided looking me in the eyes. A woman in a frilly white dress, holding the hands of two young children, glanced my direction and crossed the road, probably to keep from meeting me.

I found myself in front of a school. The sign said it was Douglass School. I couldn't remember who Douglass was, if I ever knew. And where would Mr. Scott's house be? I didn't have much of a choice except to ask people, no matter what color they were. "Excuse me," I said to a man, out walking with a woman.

The couple stopped politely. "Yes?" asked the man, adjusting his hat.

"Can you tell me where Mr. James Scott lives?"

The woman frowned disapprovingly. The man tilted his head. "Mind my asking why you want to know?"

"I can't find my uncle. Heard Mr. Scott might be able to give me a clue or two."

"Who's your uncle?"

"His name is Morris Scott."

"You from around here?"

"No, sir. St. Louis."

"Well," he said. He glanced sideways at me and coughed. Maybe he wasn't used to being called "sir" by a white person.

Then he turned around pointed further up the street. "See that house there, across the street? Big frame one on the corner?"

"Yes." I straightened up.

"You try there."

"Thank you so much."

He touched his hat, extended his arm to the woman, and resumed walking.

Filled with purpose, I walked the two blocks as quickly as I could, leaped up the steps to the wide porch, and thumped the door knocker.

I stood there for five minutes before knocking again.

No answer.

I waited about half an hour, knocking at the door on and off.

Still, no answer.

CHAPTER 24

After gobbling down some hearty navy bean soup for lunch in Mrs. McLaren's kitchen, I got ready for work—I changed into Frederick McLaren's overalls, shirt and pale-blue boxers held up with buttons, not elastic. They felt loose and strange.

I scratched my head as I walked across the back yard toward the shop. Had Silas by now told Mr. McLaren that I'd helped a black woman pump some water? Would that be cause for asking me to leave?

Mr. McLaren sat on a metal chair just inside the garage bay, the open door letting some spring sunshine light up the cluttered, dark interior.

Silas walked up at a rapid pace, his back as straight as a pole, a sour expression on his face. "This kid you took in ..." he began ...

Mr. McLaren held up a hand to stop the torrent of words as one of those fancy roadsters drove up, a powerful long car opened up to the weather. A Buick. It chugged into the driveway, driven by a well-dressed man with a cloud of gray hair, a professor who needed his spare tire pumped up. Next, a farmer in a muddy, rusty Model T needed a new spark plug.

I had a waxy rag and did my best to shine the fenders of the cars. I changed a tire, too.

I peeked under the hoods, despite Silas doing his best to stand in my way. A huge feeling of satisfaction washed over me. If I ever got back to 2019, I'd know a lot more about the cars at the car shows.

A black man in a navy-blue uniform drove up with a green roadster, a new sedan with hickory wheels. He said his employer, a Mr. Sloan, wanted the car to have more "git up and git."

"You got plenty of git-up-and-git with that big six," grunted Silas. "But I'll see what I can do." He got out his screwdriver and tinkered with the carburetor while Mr. McLaren went to my room at the back of the garage and spread some accounting sheets out on the table. The black man stood on the front lawn, squinting at the spring sun, waiting without fidgeting.

I walked up to him, holding my polishing rag. "Excuse me," I said. "I'm looking for a man named James Scott. You know him?"

"Colored man?" he asked, his eyebrows raised.

"Yes, sir."

"He go to my church, Second Baptist." He paused. "So, why you asking, if I might inquire?"

"My uncle. He's disappeared since we got to Columbia the other night on the train. But he wanted to find Mr. Scott, ask a question."

The man mused. "So, why'd your uncle disappear?"

"Wish I knew. Been looking for him high and low."

"Maybe Scotty know where he at?"

"Yes."

"Scotty ain't hiding. Just walk up Third Street, ask anybody where he live, and he'll talk to you. He works as a janitor at the college. He got a handsome family."

"Thanks," I said. I held up my rag. "Guess I got to get back to work."

"You do that."

I was doing my best to polish a bright red Stutz Bearcat when I heard a voice calling from the street, "Daily Columbia Missourian!"

It was one of those paper boys again. I dropped my rag and raced outside.

The skinny one with glasses was expertly flipping a newspaper onto the porch of the house next door. He came to the end of our driveway, grinned, and flipped it to me. I caught it and put it down. "Okay if I take a break, Mr. McLaren?" I called over my shoulder.

"Sure, son. Fifteen minutes." The answer wafted from the room behind the garage.

"Glad you got a job. So, walk with me," said the paperboy, who told me his name was Arthur. "You can see what I do." The rolled-up newspapers, tied with string, hung in a bag from his shoulder like arrows in a quiver. He pulled one out with minimal movement and flicked it to the next porch.

"Here, you try it." He pointed.

I threw the newspaper end over end, and it thumped against the house's front door before ricocheting back down to the porch floor. I grimaced.

"You'll get the hang of it if you do it much," he said. "You play baseball, right?"

"No." I shook my head. "Played some soccer when I was smaller."

"Soccer? Where all you do is kick the ball?"

I nodded my head.

"Never met anybody who played soccer before."

"It just means I'm not good at throwing."

"Here." He handed me another paper and pointed to the next porch. "Practice."

I threw it. It didn't hit the door, but, then, it didn't hit the porch either. It landed on the steps.

Next door, somebody was sitting outside, an old guy in a rocker, watching us with alert blue eyes shaded by bushy white eyebrows and wearing an odd gray cap.

Arthur elbowed me. "Mr. Conrad fought in the Civil War. He'd love to bore you to death with his war stories. About how he never stopped fighting even after they declared the war was over." Arthur tossed a paper that landed smack in the man's open hands. "That's how I give him the news every day."

"A live Civil War veteran?" I was having some trouble digesting this information. "Which side was he on?"

"He's got a gray hat. Like all the fighters from around here. Johnny Reb."

The Confederate side. I faintly remembered from school that Missouri had been pretty divided at the Civil War.

Arthur turned and jogged further up the street, passing a house with an overgrown lawn. "Ain't you got some Civil War veterans in St. Louis?"

"I guess so. Just never remembered meeting one, is all."

"Richie!" A man's voice called me from McLaren's. It was Silas. "Get back here. No slacking off."

"Gotta get back to work," I said.

"You talk different," said Arthur.

Oops.

CHAPTER 25

Since it was Saturday, we had plenty of business. Apparently, the farmers would drive into town on Saturday afternoons to shop, get things fixed, see their friends, whatever.

Late in the day, I finished polishing a car. No sooner had it left than a big blue roadster drove up, its convertible top down, a black man at the wheel. He wasn't wearing livery. Instead, he wore a regular shirt, hat, and tie, a smile, a gold wedding ring, and a bushy moustache under his nose. Did he actually own this car? I aimed to find out.

He got out and addressed Mr. McLaren, who'd come out of the back room. "Mr. McLaren," he said. "My Hupmobile here needs a quick oil change. Can you make that happen for me?"

An expression of distaste flickered across Mr. McLaren's face. But he said, "Sure thing, Mr. Scott."

I took in a sharp breath. Was this James Scott?

Silas, muttering under his breath, pulled the car into the garage and set about working on it from underneath while standing in the pit in the concrete floor.

I pulled out my rag and started rubbing the rear fender, my hands trembling. I had to figure out what to tell him. And I had to figure it out fast.

Mr. Scott watched me, an amused expression on his face. "I ain't seen you here before."

"Just started working here. You got a beautiful car." I was babbling.

His face, creased into an answering smile, reminded me of Morris. He was shorter and thinner, though, not much taller than me.

Maybe he was thirty years old, like Morris in 1969.

His eyes shone brightly. "You ain't from here."

"St. Louis."

"I'm from Chicago."

"You get this car in Chicago?"

"No indeed. Got it after I got down here." His voice rang with pride.

I bent over to rub the other fender.

"I was born here in Columbia, but pretty soon after that my family moved to New Mexico, and then to Chicago," he said.

"Richie." The voice of Silas again. Of course, working on the oil change, he'd heard every word.

Mr. Scott laid a finger across his lips and winked. I had the feeling he kind of liked breaking the rules.

I kept polishing, furiously wondering what else to say. "You need to be careful, Mr. Scott," wouldn't sound right at the moment, even if it was the truth.

Mr. Scott retreated to the front yard. Silas showed up next to me with a funnel, a can opener, and an armful of oil cans.

"You keep your trap shut," he muttered. "You know we don't talk friendly-like to them."

"Why not?" I spoke in a normal tone.

"You sap."

I didn't want Mr. McLaren to hear. So, I didn't answer.

After a few minutes, Silas slammed the hood and stepped back. "Done." He lowered himself into the driver's seat and fired up the car. Its massive engine roared at first and then purred, and he backed it into the driveway, grinning like the proud rider of a prize stallion.

I located the wind-up clock on a shelf in the garage. Five o'clock. It was time to quit work.

Mr. Scott paid Mr. McLaren, put the car into gear, and eased it on down the block.

"I can go, right, Mr. McLaren?"

"You go on. Thank you for your work, Richie."

I nodded and took off after the car. As I ran, I waved at the three newsboys.

Mr. Scott paused the car at the end of the street as if there was a stop sign there—there wasn't—and turned right. I flew around the corner after him, in time to see him pausing and then heading straight through the next intersection.

He pulled over and stopped. Perhaps he'd seen me running after him in his side mirror. In any case, I was panting hard by the time I caught up to him.

"Hey, Mr. Scott," I said between gasps.

"Want a ride, Sonny?"

"Yes, sir."

He gestured with an open palm. "Climb in." He chuckled as I opened the front door and settled in. "You know, don't you, that people around here would expect you to sit in the back, and I'd be your driver and not talk to you."

"Not me," I said. "Thanks for giving me a ride."

He grinned, nodded, and pulled an ornate silver pocket watch out of his vest pocket.

I'd seen it before.

My scalp prickled. Puzzle pieces slid into place in my head. It **was** Morris I'd bumped into in 2019. He must have been eighty years old, and he was holding that exact watch or one just like it before I knocked it out of his hand and into a million pieces.

This Mr. Scott really was the man I was looking for. He glanced at the watch. "The wife and kids are expecting me home pretty soon, but I think we got time for a little joyride in the country. You up for it?"

"Let's do it!" I couldn't help bouncing on the seat like a little kid. I'd dreamed about this at car shows. Now, here it was, happening.

The muscle car made short work of the town. After paying a toll of ten cents at a covered bridge, we cruised away from the westering sun on a gravel road, engine roaring. The speed took me, wind messing up my hair like a big invisible grandpa. The small windshield did almost nothing to keep the wind off, and that was just the way I liked it.

As the pastures and fields flew by I grinned and grinned. Mr. Scott grinned back. The wind made it too loud to talk, so I soaked up the peace of being free on the road, listening to the din of the car engine. It felt like flying, in a way that driving much faster in the twenty-first century could never do.

Soon enough, though, Mr. Scott stopped the car and turned it around in the dirt driveway of a farmhouse. Then we sped back.

We got to town and slowed down to navigate the streets. Mr. Scott turned to me. "Where can I take you, uh—?"

"Richie. Not going much of anywhere. Maybe you can let me off, just anywhere."

"Why don't you come home with me? I want you to meet my family."

"Sure!" My fist shot into the air, then I quickly pulled it down. The gesture must've looked pretty odd.

There was a pause. Now was my opportunity. "Mr. Scott, you need to be careful," I said.

"Why's that?" He expertly cranked the steering wheel to turn a corner.

"Don't do anything you'd regret."

He laughed. "Son, that's the way I live my life."

"I had to tell you that. I just have a feeling you need to hear it."

He looked over at me, an eyebrow raised. We rolled down Broadway.

I'd delivered the message. Was it enough?

We were threading our way through a crowd of Model T's, mule-drawn wagons, and assorted automobiles. Some people looked at us. One woman elbowed the woman walking next to her to point us out.

Who cared if these people thought I was breaking the rules? They were stupid rules, and they cast a long shadow into the future, a shadow that affected my friend Morris nearly fifty years from now. In fact, the shadow stretched like a stain over hundreds of years.

On the Scotts' front porch, a slender woman came out of the front door. Mr. Scott took swift strides up the porch steps to kiss her and turned to me. "This is my wife, Mrs. Scott. Gertrude, this is Richie, a kid working at McLaren's Garage who loves cars and wanted a ride."

"Pleased to meet you."

At the doorway, a rich, meaty aroma drew us further into the dim interior, where a single electric bulb illuminated the front hall.

Mr. Scott smiled at me over his shoulder as he stepped into the living room. He beckoned me with his head. "Come meet my kids, Richie."

Two teenagers sitting on the sofa rose, a boy and a girl. The girl wore her hair in two braided pigtails, pulled tight. "Hello," she said shyly, straightening her loose-fitting dress. Maybe she was a bit older than me.

"This is Anna," he said, bending to kiss her on the head.

Anna. Miss Anna. I'd met her as an older woman. A shiver ran up my spine.

"And Harrison." He patted the boy on the shoulder. Morris's father was a little younger than me, slender and spindly, but already nearly as tall as his father. He looked inquiringly at Mr. Scott, as if asking how to respond to such an unusual person appearing in their living room.

"Richie's from St. Louis, and I gave him a ride in the Hupmobile."

At the table, he asked a blessing. The five of us ate meat, gravy, potatoes, and green beans in the light of a simple chandelier.

"I got a brother who stays in St. Louis," Mr. Scott said. "Took the train to see him once before I got married. Went to a ball game and a jazz club, had a great time."

"Why'd you move here?"

"My mother. She's starting to get old, and she came here a while back. Needs a son around."

"You got the car fixed up, James?" Mrs. Scott asked Mr. Scott.

"Sure. McLarens' took care of it." He winked at me. "All set. Now I can take the family for a Sunday drive—"

Someone beat on the front door. Boom! Boom! Boom!

"Police!" said a muffled male voice. "Open up!"

Fear flashed across Mrs. Scott's face, and Mr. Scott rose. "I'll answer it."

His family followed him to the door. I hung back, scolding myself. Too late. My warning was too late.

"You Mr. Scott?"

"Yessir."

"There's been an attack involving a young white lady, yesterday afternoon between three and four o'clock."

"I was at work. I haven't done anything wrong, sir." His voice was respectful, and it trembled slightly.

"We'd like you to come in for questioning. I see you fit the description, Mr. Scott, a colored man with a moustache."

"Plenty of men have moustaches."

"A Charlie Chaplin moustache, like yours—we'll talk to you and to others."

"James!" Mrs. Scott's shriek shattered the silence in the hall.

"Now, come right along."

"No!" Her voice cracked and broke.

I heard the click of handcuffs.

"Don't take my Daddy!" Harrison yelled.

"Daddy!" Anna's voice shrilled.

"No! Let him go!" I stepped forward in time to see the door slam, leaving a weeping Mrs. Scott. The two kids clung to her.

CHAPTER 26

Back at McLaren's, I spent a restless night tossing and turning, dreaming. Cold, cold floors and granite. When I woke up, my blanket had fallen off the cot. It was Sunday morning.

The McLarens knew about my little joy ride, I was sure. But Mrs. McLaren didn't say anything as she placed a plate of scrambled eggs in front of me and then vanished. I was guzzling a glass of foaming warm milk, when I heard a chair scrape, and then another. Footsteps came my way. I stood. Time to bolt.

No, I wasn't going to run. I made myself turn to the doorway as Mr. McLaren came through it.

"Richie," he said. His tone was flat. "Let's go out on the front porch. Silas is out there."

"Yes, sir."

Outside, the crazy loud sounds of springtime birds in the morning filled my ears.

"You did a good job for me yesterday," Mr. McLaren said. "I appreciate that. But then, I heard you accepted a ride from Mr. Scott and also hospitality for dinner."

"Yes, sir."

"I don't know why you don't know the local customs, Richie. You're from St. Louis. That's not so far away. I've been there. People there are like people here."

If he only knew how much. Even in 2019, people didn't mix races much in St. Louis. The black folks lived on the north side, and the white folks didn't. And the white folks never went to the north side. They complained it was dangerous.

Silas cleared his throat. "I think this boy is a Communist immigrant. He don't know the local customs. He sings rude songs. He don't understand the lingo. And we don't understand his." He glared. "He certainly ain't deserving your hospitality, Mr. McLaren. I didn't get no hospitality like that when I was a kid in St. Louis on my own, that's for sure."

Mr. McLaren rolled up a sleeve. "So, what is it, Richie? Why are you making friends with the colored folks?"

"I have a friend," I said. "He's African-American. I mean, colored."

"You're not talking about Mr. Scott."

"No, sir. His name is Morris."

He ran his hand through his thinning hair. "If you want to keep this behavior up and live on your own, I got no problem with that. You're grown, you make your own decisions. But I do have a problem if you keep this up and you work for me."

"What's that?"

"I'm in business. People in this town follow the rules. If you don't, the word will get around, and I'll lose customers."

I didn't want to hurt Mr. McLaren, and I hadn't thought about the point he was making. He and Mrs. McLaren weren't rich, I could see that. And they were generous to me.

Mrs. McLaren came through the front screen door, clearly upset. "Bill! I looked everywhere, and it's like I told you. It's gone!"

He turned and studied her. "Your wedding ring is not gone."

"Yes, it is. I had it next to the sink. I put it there when I was washing the dishes."

"I don't think anyone took it."

"Where else could it be? I don't know where it is."

Silas indicated me with a tilt of his head.

"Bill! I don't know where my wedding ring is."

"I didn't take it," I said, my heart sinking.

"Communist, Irish," said Silas.

"Go ahead, search me."

Mr. McLaren shook his head.

"You can see you're causing trouble for me. I don't know if you took it or not, Richie, but I'm going to have to ask you to leave."

I sagged against the rough brick wall of the house. After a deep breath, I answered him. "Yes, sir." I took off down the steps and down the block.

Once again, I was homeless. But this time I had no gun, no tent, and no sleeping bag. They thought I was a thief. Again.

———◆●◆———

My thoughts turned to Mr. Scott in jail. People pointed me toward the tall, domed courthouse just off Broadway, and a less-than-imposing stone structure next to it: the Columbia jailhouse with attached police station.

I stood under a high barred window: "Mr. Scott? You in there?"

"He's down the way," said a rough voice in response. "No window. Who says they want him?"

"Richie. Tell him I was asking after him."

"Okay, kid."

Would he get the message?

I roamed around the town all morning, and by afternoon was getting sore feet. I was hungry. What could I do? If only

I had a fishhook and some line. Where would I fish, though? The creeks around here were sewage canals.

As night fell, I sat on a bench near the jail. I'd keep Mr. Scott company in my own way.

It was too cold to sleep, so after a while I paced back and forth under the jailhouse window. I heard an occasional exclamation in there, but no voice I could tell was Mr. Scott's.

Around midnight, a policeman asked me what I was doing. He listened to my tale of losing my uncle and brought me into the police station, where he gave me a blanket and let me sleep in a stuffed chair. In the morning, he gave me some coffee before he sent me on my way.

CHAPTER 27

Monday morning. Six days. What could I do to help Mr. Scott? I needed to keep myself alive, if I was going to do him any good, and I hadn't had food since breakfast yesterday.

I could ask the Scotts for breakfast.

Soon, I stood on their doorstep and knocked. The wispy moisture of morning lifted from their lawn in the strengthening sunlight.

Mrs. Scott answered the door.

"I, uh, got fired yesterday," I said. "So I haven't eaten."

"You got fired on account of us?" She wore what must be her teacher clothes, a white blouse and dark skirt.

"It's not your fault. My choice. Anyway, they also accused me of stealing something, but I didn't."

"That happened to my niece Bessie," she said. "McLarens accused her of stealing, so she lost her job doing their laundry on Mondays." She shook her head and opened the door wide for me. "Come in, I'll feed you. They just can't keep track of their jewelry, that's all."

"I hung out at the courthouse square last evening," I said as I took a bite of the pancakes she gave me.

She nodded. "They let our pastor into the jail. He says Scotty's in a cell with two other colored men. He wasn't anywhere near that white girl when that attack happened. He's hoping to be released soon. Somebody at work will be able to say he was there."

Harrison and Anna were dressed for school, he in those short pants and long socks, she in a yellow baggy dress. I guess you can't take a day off from school just because your father gets put in jail.

They all headed out, and I launched on a ramble around downtown.

I could do some investigating. Where did Mr. Scott work, anyway? Had someone told me?

Finally, it came to me—the African-American driver of the car who came for service to McLaren's had said Mr. Scott was a janitor at the college.

But it was a big college, and it would take a while to ask around.

I walked the five or six blocks to Mizzou and approached a student outside the library, a guy sitting on a bench reading a really fat book. The midafternoon sun lit up the blooming dogwood tree that hung over us.

"Do you know a black, I mean, colored man who works here named James Scott?" I asked.

The guy gave me a perplexed look. "Sorry, no idea who that is."

"He's a janitor."

He shook his head. "I, uh, don't pay much attention to the help."

I asked two more students, same result. Then I went into the library and asked the librarian. "That's not our custodian in this building," she said.

Tried the Journalism School and a dormitory.

Clearly, I needed more information. And I had no internet.

How did people ever get anything done in 1923?

Under the window at the jail, I asked the men in there to ask Mr. Scott where he worked, Richie wanted to know.

The answer came back. "He's a janitor at the college."

"But," I said, "where at the college?"

By this time, an argument had broken out in the cells. No one was interested in playing my little game of pass-the-question.

***

I went off in search of my only other friends, the newspaper boys. Maybe they could help me with food and shelter. Being homeless was no picnic.

I came back to the McLarens' neighborhood and stood next to the stack of newspapers, watching the chickens across the street look for bugs. Clouds moved to cover the sun.

The trio showed up. "Hey," I said. "I'm wondering if you've heard any news."

Arthur hurried to introduce his two friends, Larry, the chubby one, and Willie, the short one. "'Course we've heard news," said Larry. "That's our job."

"What kind of news do you want?" asked Arthur.

"About an attack on a white girl a few days ago, and them looking for a black man who did it," I said.

"You mean 'colored,'" said Willie. "You Saint Louis people gotta learn our way of talking, Richie."

"Okay, colored," I said. At least they weren't asking me to say the n-word, which I'd heard plenty of times as white people talked.

"So, why do you want to know about this case?" asked Willie.

"Just want to know."

The four of us picked up copies of the paper and scanned the front page.

Arthur stabbed the lower right corner. "There."

We examined the brief notice, which ran under this headline: "Attack on Fourteen-Year-Old White Girl Last Friday."

It read, "There was no announcement from police today regarding the search for the negro who made an attack on a fourteen-year-old white girl last Friday." That was it. It was short and sweet. And puzzling.

"What's that mean for Mr. Scott?" I muttered.

"Mr. Scott? He the colored man who gave you a ride the other day?" asked Arthur.

"Yeah. The police picked him up for questioning because he had a Charlie Chaplin moustache. That was Saturday. He's still in jail."

Willie rattled the paper. "I get my news from the newspaper, like everybody else."

"'Course, there's several newspapers in town," said Larry. "And we only see this one. Could be more news out there."

"He has an alibi. He was at work. They could have released him after they questioned him. But they didn't."

"Say," said Arthur, "I didn't see you working at McLaren's today."

"Got fired yesterday. They thought I stole a ring. But I didn't, of course."

"So, where you staying?"

I gestured with open hands. "I was just walking around last night, until a policeman took pity on me and gave me a blanket and a stuffed chair in the police station for a little while."

The three of them looked at each other. "I know," said Arthur. "You can stay in the shed behind Mrs. Little's house.

She's gone to live with her son, and the house is empty. The shed just has a few tools in it, I bet. At least it'll keep you dry if it rains."

"I can get a blanket for you," said Larry.

"I'll get you a ham hock—or maybe chicken livers," said Willie.

"Can't thank you guys enough," I said. I was that hungry.

The shed had a dirt floor barely big enough for me to stretch out, with a shovel and a hoe poking my shoulder. But it was better than a bench at the courthouse or a chair in the police station.

I had trouble falling asleep.

Mr. Scott had five days to live.

CHAPTER 28

I felt stiff the next morning, Tuesday, but I made my way over to campus. There a policeman found me. "I hear you've been asking a lot of people a lot of questions."

"Yes, sir."

"We don't want homeless, pickpockets, thieves, on this campus," he said smoothly. "Now you get out of here."

I left, of course. But how was I supposed to help Mr. Scott? I didn't want to get on the wrong side of the law, so all day I just laid low. In the evening, I went in search of news.

The daylight faded as I walked north toward the Scotts', and the wind smelled like rain. Kids were out in yards, people on porches. I tried to ignore the odor of the creek not far away. When I leaped up the steps to the wide porch and thumped the door knocker, it looked like no one migh be home, with no lights on inside. But lights in 1923 were far dimmer than what I was used to.

I stood there for five minutes. No answer. Rain began to patter on the roof. I dragged myself off the sheltered porch and down the steps.

There were no streetlights in this part of town. I walked quickly back on the dirt street, now mud, trying not to slip. I passed the school and crossed the stinking creek on a small bridge. Why didn't I wear my jacket?

The rain let up.

Shadows materialized beside me. Three of them. All taller than me.

The hair lifted on the back of my neck.

"You got that money? Give it to me." Rough hands pushed me, and I nearly fell.

"I don't have any—"

"Hand it over."

"Where you got it?"

I pulled both overall pockets inside out. The white fabric was only somewhat visible in the darkness. Frederick McLaren's handkerchief fluttered to the ground.

"Cough it up."

"You got it there somewhere."

A blow hit my jaw.

I called out: "Help me, somebody!"

I swung out with my right as hard as I could, but connected with air.

Wham! Another blow struck my ear. I staggered and fell into the mud. I couldn't get up.

The wind knocked out of me; I just lay there. Soon, hands lifted me up out of the mud. A vehicle had come up beside me. "Open your eyes." A gruff white man was speaking. "You hear me?"

"Yeah," I mumbled, blinking in the light of the headlamps, throbbing pain in my jaw making it hard to talk. I could see now that there were two cops in front of me, both white.

"Somebody 'round here heard a commotion," said the taller policeman.

"You get an eyeful of whoever done this to you?"

"No, sir."

I washed the mud off at the tiny one-faucet sink in the small police station bathroom. It was as good a bath as I'd had since my hot shower. The water was shockingly cold.

"Richard Roberts, vagrant," the taller cop said, when I returned to his desk, still shivering. "Stealing. I have a warrant for your arrest."

I turned my pockets inside out again. Nothing was there, of course.

"Give me the address of wherever you've been sleeping the past couple of nights. I need to get a warrant to search it."

I gave him rough directions.

"You'll be staying in the jail overnight, and we'll talk to a judge in the morning."

It would be Wednesday morning. My birthday was Sunday. Time was slipping away.

"You don't understand, somebody's going to get killed. He's going to die." I tugged at the taller man's arm, my voice rising.

"What are you talking about?"

"They're going to kill him."

"Who?" said the shorter cop.

"People."

"People?"

I pointed at him. "You."

"Me?"

"That's what I'm trying to tell you."

"Not me," said the shorter man.

"Who's going to get killed?" asked the other.

"He's crazy," the shorter one broke in.

"Take him to the jail."

My voice grew even more shrill. "You're going to kill him. He's going to die."

"Who are you talking about?"

"I have to stop it."

"Stop what?"

"That's enough. Take the boy to the jail."

"What are you talking about, kid? What are you saying?"

"Lock him up."

"Crazy kid. Take him away."

CHAPTER 29

The cops settled me alone in a four-person cell surrounded by brick walls. My jaw still throbbed from the mugging, but I tried to ignore it. One side of the tiny room was open to the hall but barred. I wasn't alone. I could hear talking and exclamations down the hall.

"James Scott? You here?" I called out.

"Don't know him," said a voice, finally, to my right. "You the one they booted us out of that cell for? A kid?"

"I know Mr. Scott is here somewhere."

"I'm here." It was his voice. In a cell just to my left. Bingo! I gripped my cell bars.

"I've been asking, trying to get you an alibi. But I don't know exactly where you work."

"Medical school," said a lower voice. His cellmate, maybe.

"Big brick building on the edge of campus." That was Mr. Scott.

"Thanks. I'll work on that." An idea lit up my thoughts. "I know. Maybe we could pop you out of here, put you on a train ... to Chicago or something. New York, some place."

"Richie, Richie. Whatever it is that's coming. I'll just take it."

I shuffled my feet and kicked at the floor-to-ceiling bars. I didn't want to be here, and I didn't want him to be here.

"You, kid. Be quiet." In a couple of minutes, a guard completed his walk down the hall, jingling his keys, and most of the lights went off. Some of the prisoners continued to swear and talk, but I didn't hear Mr. Scott again.

Wednesday morning, I had a jailhouse breakfast—bitter coffee—and a judge reviewed the evidence in my case, or lack of it, and let me go. I dusted the caked mud off my clothes and headed back toward my shack, feeling desperate enough to look for acorns. But then the news boys brought me some bread, an apple, and taffy, and I helped Larry and Arthur with their paper routes.

Around noon, I made it over to campus, but a campus policeman found me in short order and sent me away.

Late in the day, I set out for the Scotts' again. Down Broadway, globed streetlights stood like sentinels on steel posts. I turned north on Third Street and immediately stepped into the darkness and dirt streets. I let my eyes adjust until I could see the road in the faint light from people's living rooms and the occasional front porch fixture. I tried to keep my weight on the balls of my feet in case I needed to run.

Harrison answered the door at the Scott's, his skinny frame silhouetted against the bare bulb in the front hall so I couldn't really see his face.

I could tell he was scared. He kept gulping, and his eyes were opened wide. "I thought you was the police," he told me.

I shook my head. "You seen any more of the police?"

"No." He gestured toward the living room. "Come in and talk to Miss Gertrude."

I recalled she and Mr. Scott had only been married a couple of years.

Sitting on the sofa, Mrs. Scott held Anna's hand on one side and the hand of an older woman I didn't know on the other. "Richie," she said, indicating the older woman. "This is Miss Sarah Brown, Mr. Scott's mother."

"Pleased to meet you, ma'am."

Her face was somber. A small woman, Miss Sarah's gray hair was knotted into a bun. "You that new friend of my son's? The young 'uns told me about you."

We talked about St. Louis for a little bit, and I tried my best to not speak "different" or say anything that would sound really weird to them. But they were waiting for Reverend Casten, not me—and until he arrived, they were clearly on edge.

He turned out to be a short, thick-set African-American man with a large moustache and a take-charge air. Harrison introduced me. The Reverend didn't bat an eye at the color of my skin. "You his friend?"

"Yes, sir."

"Glad to hear it. I'm his pastor. Maybe you can help him out somehow."

"I'd be glad to."

"We all need friends."

He sat in an upholstered chair and cleared his throat. "I met with our man Scotty at the jail a little while ago. He hasn't been charged—nobody's been charged with anything. They're investigating, got a reward out for anyone who can tell them where he was at a little after three on Friday.

"That reward's getting too big. More folks is getting interested in catching the man who did this, so they're contributing. Eleven hundred twenty-five dollars."

Harrison whistled. "That's enough to get people to invent stories, just for the money."

That was a lot of money, considering that you could buy a Coke for a nickel.

"They suggest he attacked Regina Almstedt, age fourteen, under Stewart Bridge last Friday afternoon between three and four."

Anna swallowed.

"The attacker told her he was looking to get revenge on the white man who stole his wife, so he was after a white woman."

"My son is happily married," said Miss Sarah, "even has Anna, a daughter the same age."

"Daddy wouldn't attack nobody," said Anna.

"They're looking at him because he's got that Charlie Chaplin moustache," said Reverend Casten.

I guess I had seen a picture of the funny little tramp, but my father would have known more about him than me.

"A Charlie Chaplin moustache? Are they crazy, dragging him in because of a moustache like Charlie Chaplin?" I asked.

"If I knew the police were looking for me, I'd shave that moustache off real quick," said Harrison. "I know that the guy who really did it ain't got no moustache no more, I can guarantee that."

"Yeah," I said. "You gotta be right."

"How's James feeling?" asked Mrs. Scott.

Reverend Casten shook his head. "Pretty down. He keeps telling them he's innocent. But the girl identified Scotty today."

Mrs. Scott drew in a sharp breath.

"Miss Gertrude, I got to tell you, we need to pray," said Reverend Casten. "And we need to get him a lawyer. I'm looking at hiring Emmett Anderson for him. President of the county bar association. A white man, of course. Best lawyer in the county."

Tears glistened in her eyes, and she nodded.

"We'll have him sign over the Hupmobile to Mr. Anderson. There isn't anything else to sign over."

She nodded again.

"I also want to invite George Vaughn to join the team. He's a heavy-hitter colored lawyer from St. Louis. NAACP man. I'll ask him to stand by, be ready to come on down here in case Scotty is officially arrested."

Mrs. Scott burst into tears.

"These two can clear an innocent man. I'm sure of it."

Anna and Mrs. Brown rubbed Mrs. Scott's back for comfort.

All this bad news made my shoulder slump like I'd picked up a heavy, heavy load. Finally, I asked, "What can I do?"

"Well, keep your eyes and ears open in the white community for me." Reverend Casten said. "That would be a help. Get any information to me at my house. I'll show you where it is."

"Yes, sir," I said, glad to have something to do.

He stood, fished something out of his pocket, and opened his hand. The pocket watch. "I nearly forgot. Harrison, your father wanted you to have this. There's no place to keep it safe at the jail." He handed it to Harrison.

"Let's pray," Reverend Casten's prayer was to the point, short: "Lord, we pray you will save Scotty. Help us to do whatever we need to do. Enable us and strengthen us. And him. Amen."

"Thank you," Harrison whispered. He placed his father's watch carefully on the mantel.

I cleared my throat after Reverend Casten stood to leave, "Sir, I'm not from here, and I don't really know where I can go and listen for information that would be helpful for Mr. Scott."

He clapped me on the shoulder. "Go where the men go. Hang out on Broadway. If people are congregating, go congregate with them. You could even go where there's drinking, but be careful. Used to be, you'd be underage for drinking. But now with Prohibition, everybody's underage, I guess." He chuckled.

I'd heard about Prohibition; although drinking was outlawed , everybody did it anyway.

"But you'll need to be careful," he said.

We walked out together into the murk.

CHAPTER 30

There was no mention of the attack on Regina Almstedt in the *Daily Evening Missourian* next day, Thursday, my newsboy friends determined.

My time on campus had been brief before I was asked to leave again, so I helped the newsboys deliver newspapers. Then in the late afternoon, I wandered over to Broadway and sauntered up and down the street, which was nowhere near as crowded as it usually was on a Saturday.

I nearly ran into a young woman wearing a bell-shaped hat and a long loose dress belted around the hips. She lifted her eyebrows and formed an "o" with her lipsticked mouth as she passed me, but she didn't say anything. I passed a lunch counter with a small handwritten sign in the window—"No colored."

Shaking my head, I walked north on a brick-paved street and spied a group of white men talking loudly.

The place was a feed store for farmers. A couple of wagons with teams were hitched at its rail, and three Model T's stood parked in the street.

"We got to spare that poor young girl exposure at a trial," said a man wearing overalls.

"You're right, Barkwell. Young ladies are too delicate for that."

"She's a professor's daughter," said another. "Almstet or something. I hear he's been talking to the police for her. As he should be."

I thought I'd found the sort of group Reverend Casten was looking for. I eased into the shadow of a nearby doorway and made myself as invisible as possible.

"You sure they got the right man?" asked someone.

"She identified him. Fair and square."

"He's too big for his britches." With a shock I realized it was Silas's voice. "He's from Chicago. Rides around in that *Hup*mobile." He accented the "Hup" part. "Shoulda known he'd be powerful stupid."

I froze. I knew they were talking about Mr. Scott.

Conversation veered to other topics: the weather, finding help for planting, a sick mule, too many immigrants turning the cities upside-down. After a while, the group dispersed, and finally I emerged to an empty street. I walked back to Broadway slowly, in case anyone had seen me.

At the Scott's that evening, Reverend Casten sat in the living room in the upholstered chair. He was praying with the family for peace and justice. When they were finished, I told them what I'd heard and seen.

"It's getting dangerous," said Reverend Casten. "We can see that. I was just telling the family here that it's looking very likely Scotty will be charged. I've already engaged Mr. Anderson as the attorney, and he's interviewing people who can provide an alibi. I know we'll be able to show that Scotty was indeed at work at the time of the crime." He shook his head in disgust. "Of course, the police weren't looking for alibi witnesses. They were only looking for someone to claim that Scotty, Mr. Scott, was guilty."

"Oh, man," I muttered. But at least somebody else was now asking around for an alibi witness.

Reverend Casten went on, "That big reward did do its evil work. Somebody come forward to claim that Scotty was seen near the scene of the crime at 4:15—that would be just after the incident."

Tears trickled down Mrs. Scott's face. Anna put her arm around her and gave her a hug.

———————◆●◆———————

The next afternoon, Friday, the newsboys and I opened the stack of newspapers and scanned the headlines.

"Here!" I pointed at the crowded front page. "Here's what I'm looking for. 'Action in Negro Attack Case is Expected Soon.'"

I continued to read aloud. "While there has been no announcement from the city or county authorities, evidence has been piled up against a certain negro suspected of the attack against a fourteen-year-old girl made last Friday afternoon.

"... At 4:30 o'clock, charges had not been filed and no official announcement of the identity of the negro had been made."

Arthur adjusted his glasses. "Those charges are going to be made tonight."

"What do you know about filing charges?" asked Willie.

"I want to be a lawyer, don't I?" Arthur asked with a hurt expression. "I follow these things."

"What's that mean, filing charges?" Larry didn't know anything. I didn't know much more.

"That's what they do before they set a trial for somebody. File the charges so that everybody knows what they are, and the lawyers can get their cases ready." Arthur bobbed his head.

I let out a big sigh.

Arthur shook his head. "Do you think he did it?"

"No. I don't think he did it at all. But he needs to clear his name," I said.

I made my way over to the university as night fell. Ban or no, I'd been sent from the future to save Mr. Scott. I had to work on the alibi some more.

I found the brick medical school building. It was locked.

I dragged one foot behind the other on my way back. He had only two days to live now. Unless I could stop it somehow.

CHAPTER 31

Saturday, the town buzzed. All the country folks had arrived to shop and visit. I took a quick walk up Broadway mid-morning and heard snatches of conversation about the man who'd been charged. People were waving the morning paper at each other, the **Columbia Daily Tribune**. They talked about the fact that the girl had identified James Scott from a lineup.

At the university, I found the medical school and this time, entered through an unlocked door. My footsteps echoed on the linoleum floor in the hallway as I looked for someone, anyone, to question.

I needed a white person, whose word might carry weight. Looking through a frosted glass pane in an office door, I could see the blurry outline of a pale person in a white shirt sitting at a desk.

A youngish man with a trimmed beard sat there examining some photographs. He looked up, eyebrow raised when he heard my knock, and I tried to introduce myself as politely as I could. "Would you happen to have seen James Scott here last Friday between three and four-thirty in the afternoon?"

The man paused and then leaned back, sucking on an unlit pipe. "You're trying to help him out, huh?"

"Yes, sir."

"He's your friend?"

"Yes, sir."

He shook his head and chuckled. "I can't say as I saw him then. I'm sorry. But I wish you the best in your search, young man."

"Thank you, sir."

"Not sure you should be here."

I continued down the hall, toward the loud clatter of a typewriter coming from the end office.

I knocked, but there was no response. I pushed the door open. A woman sat very upright in an office chair, ignoring me as she typed away. Then she looked up, and the clatter ceased.

"Yes? May I help you?"

I repeated my request.

She appeared annoyed. "Who is James Scott?"

"One of the janitors here."

She shook her head. "Sorry, I never notice those people. You'll have to ask someone else."

"Yes, ma'am."

On the next floor up, I questioned two more people, and on the top floor, I found four working in labs. None of them could help me.

There was no one else there to ask.

Shoulders sagging, feet weighing a ton each, I dragged myself back to the courthouse.

Later that afternoon, the newsboys and I had something to read in the paper. Mr. Scott had pled not guilty, and his trial was set for May 21. No alibi was mentioned.

Walking back downtown, I noted the swelling crowds on Broadway.

I sat down on the bench near the jail and watched and waited. It was night.

"Justice is afoot," one man called to another across the street.

"That's what I wanted to hear!" was the answering call.

It sounded like a threat to me, and I ran all the way to the Scotts' house.

Harrison answered the door. I told him there was talk on Broadway, and he flinched.

"Any news on the alibi?" I asked.

"Yes. Mr. Anderson has been able to find two white people so far who will testify that they saw him at work at roughly the time of the attack. One at 3:10. One at 3:45."

I grinned and punched the air above me. He'd done what I couldn't. "Is there any way to get that into the newspapers? Soon?"

He shook his head. "I don't know. Reverend Casten and Mr. Anderson are in charge. Also, the NAACP lawyer from St. Louis—George Vaughn—is coming on the train, due in just a little while ago. They're all meeting somewhere now."

I frowned. I was nearly out of time. Tomorrow was April 29.

"Pop told Reverend Casten that one of his cellmates, a colored man named Ollie Watson, told him he was Regina's attacker. Ollie attacked a black girl a week earlier, or at least he's accused of it—that's why he's in jail. Ollie told Pop he'd shaved off his moustache so he wouldn't get picked up for Regina too." Disgust filled his voice. "Now if we could get the police to listen to that."

"We need to tell the police."

We began running, but when we got to the station, Harrison wouldn't come in. Inside, the report spilled from my lips, how Ollie Watson had confessed to the crime to Mr. Scott, and how Ollie said he'd shaved his moustache off.

A block away, a shout went up, and I heard glass shattering. Something was happening out there.

I tried to tell the officer how important this was, but he told me he couldn't help me.

"We got a disturbance on our hands," he said. "Come back tomorrow." He shoved me out of the way as he emerged from the doorway, holding a nightstick in his hand, and headed toward the noise on the street.

I coiled my fists in frustration, standing by myself outside the rickety screen door at the police station. I was forced out of the way as three more cops emerged and strode toward the street. I couldn't find Harrison outside.

I stood for what seemed like hours. Then I looked at the clock. April 29 was arriving in one hour.

CHAPTER 32

A crowd gathered at the county courthouse. I hung back and watched as a group of twenty-five or thirty people ebbed and flowed around the big-pillared building and the jail next to it. Faint streetlights in the distance showed me they were nearly all men, many clad in overalls. On the fringes were a few black faces, watching.

I'd come to stop this. But I didn't know how.

A voice boomed from the confusion. "Come on! He's in here!"

The crowd rushed to the jailhouse door and began pounding on it.

Two uniformed men appeared on the porch, standing under the dim porch light. "Men, men, please calm down. It's time to stop this nonsense and go home." It was the sheriff speaking, I could see from his distinctive badge outlined in the light.

"This man needs to stand trial," called out the man beside him. "No shortcuts. This is America. With liberty and justice for all."

Someone else called out, "Justice! Summary justice, that's the kind we got tonight."

"You all need to go home," yelled the sheriff.

The crowd snarled. "Just let us at him. You know we ain't going to leave until we got him." Several of them waved ropes and pistols.

A group of young men and women raced in from a party somewhere, dressed for dancing. Several of them brandished bottles filled with liquid. But when they saw the ropes and pistols, they paused and retreated to the back of the crowd. After a while, they continued joshing with each other, laughing, drinking more. Meanwhile the men surrounding the jail pounded on the doors.

More and more townspeople and students gathered to watch—young and old, men and women, and even some children. They ran in on foot, and they came in cars, many of them big and fancy cars. Soon the crowd and the vehicles filled the square and the lawn around the courthouse, and their voices and laughter filled my ears.

"This is how we deal with 'em," I heard a man tell a boy who couldn't have been more than five. "Learn your lesson, son."

I stepped forward. "What if he's innocent?" I shouted. "He needs a trial. A fair trial." But my words got swallowed up in the general roar as the door on the other side of the jail gave way. The crowd surged forward and away from me.

I followed them around the building, where the crowd clogged a dark open doorway.

The sheriff and another man stood near me. "They'll never get past that inner door," said the sheriff to his companion. "It's like Fort Knox in there."

The other man nodded. "We don't got nothing to worry about."

Loud thwacks of hammer on metal began. Apparently, there was a metal gate inside that might stop them. I took heart.

A pair of cops stood not far away arms crossed confidently. They weren't trying to stop the proceedings either.

Would the metal gate hold? I held my breath.

After five minutes, the pounding stopped.

"A torch! We need an acetylene torch!" Voices spilled out of the dark doorway.

"A torch! A torch!" chanted the crowd.

"I got one, I'll go get it!" A man hurried off to one of the parked cars and left.

What was Mr. Scott thinking through all of this? I cringed for him.

One of the mobsters looked at me and said, "Hey, kid, if you can't take it, go home. What you doing here, anyway?"

"Hoping for justice," I said. "But not seeing it."

He nodded. "Just wait."

My cheeks burned. He thought I was on his side.

A group of men arrived with two cylindrical tanks, not too big to carry, and some hoses and metal wands. They entered the doorway. I heard fumbling and swearing in the darkness.

"They'll never get it open," said the voice of one of two cops. He stood there, arms crossed.

"Nah. Not a chance," said the other cop.

I closed my eyes when a bright blueish light flared out from the opening, making a whooshing noise. It was a pinpoint of blue fire, too hot to look at. What was it doing to the metal gate?

After a minute of whooshing, I heard a loud clang, greeted by a shout. The door inside gave way. The blue light went out.

The crowd outside pressed into the opening. I heard murmurs. "It's dark in here." "Can't see nothing." "Quit pushing." "Light that torch again to burn off this lock." "Which one is Scott?"

The men surged forward, and I heard cries of "Got him!" and other abusive words as they brought him down the hall and out of the jail. As the noisy crowd outside surged toward him, he fell. Those around him grabbed his arms and lifted him up.

"Don't drag me," he said. "I will go. But I am innocent."

And where were the two cops? Lost in the general darkness and noise. They certainly weren't saying anything now, at least that I could hear.

Mr. Scott stood, head held high, outside the jail under the jailer's porch light. Already they'd punched and kicked him, and one eye was swollen shut.

"Take him to Stewart's Bridge!" came a loud voice.

Was that Silas speaking?

I looked for the speaker and found Silas out in the crowd, his stooped, slender frame visible in the porch light.

Someone else yelled, "Let's get going! They're calling up the militia!"

A voice answered with a belly laugh. "Most of those militia people are right here with us!"

Were the two cops part of it too?

Mr. Scott was without a friend in this mob.

No. That wasn't true. I was there, and I was Mr. Scott's friend. I'd defend him to my last breath—or his.

Someone looped a rope around Mr. Scott's neck and tugged.

I moved in close and threw one arm around him, supporting him as they pulled him off balance. "It's Richie," I said.

"Richie," he murmured. "I'm so sorry ... that you have to see this ... my friend."

"I'm not going to let them do it." We were running to keep up.

He shook his head and took in a ragged breath. "Go home, Richie. Be safe."

I noticed a skinny young man beside us. A college student with a hat, white shirt, tan pants. He carried a slender notepad.

"Charles Nutter, *Columbia Evening Missourian*," he said to the two of us.

"Ah," I said. So, this was the one behind the stories we'd read in the afternoon newspaper.

"Richard Roberts," I said. "From St. Louis."

Nutter nodded.

"I'm innocent," Mr. Scott said in a louder voice.

"Shut up." The burly men at the other end of the rope swore at him and jerked the rope. Mr. Scott fell to his knees and then to his side and was dragged forward. Amid a hail of abuse from the men around us, Nutter and I pulled him up. His face and side must be bleeding, but I couldn't see in the dark. Soon, I got a good look at his bruised face as we passed a Broadway streetlamp. Some of his teeth had been knocked out, and he bled from nose and ears.

Many of the revelers raced with us through the streets, shouting and laughing. Others took to vehicles, honked repeatedly, and led the awful parade. They acted as if it was a terrific party. I just wanted to throw up.

After fifteen minutes of this wretched journey, we reached the bridge over the large ravine I'd found in my first exploration of the town. For a second there was quiet, and I heard a banjo player not far away singing.

In the streetlights, I could see that the long bridge was crowded. The dark ravine beneath us plainly served as a full amphitheater. Cries and shouts came from below.

What did I remember was down there? Scrubby trees. A railroad track. The sewage stream. In fact, I could smell it.

The rope wasn't long enough. Someone went to get another one.

Three imposing men now stood on the bridge next to Mr. Scott—one the uniformed sheriff. "Don't do this," called the sheriff to the crowd. "All I need is a few volunteers. Help me get this man to safety."

"Forget it," shouted several men from below.

"I'm Judge Collier," said another of the men. "I tell you, you will regret this. Let this man go, and let the wheels of justice turn."

"Summary justice!" yelled someone in the mob.

"You're behaving like vigilantes," hollered the judge.

The third man took his turn, speaking loudly and forcefully. "You all know me as the prosecutor in this case. I ask you now to let me do my job and give this man a trial."

"Summary justice!" repeated someone, then several men, then a shout from the crowd.

Mr. Scott raised his voice. "I'm an innocent man," he said. "I have a fifteen-year-old daughter of my own. You have the wrong person."

His words were met with catcalls.

"My cellmate," he called out, "this afternoon told me he did this. His wife and him had been having some trouble, like the girl said the man who attacked her told her about. He shaved off his moustache first thing."

"Over with him!"

"My wife never has had trouble with me. Go down and see her. I can prove my innocence."

More catcalls. Louder: "Over with him!"

A distinguished-looking man with white hair elbowed his way to the front of the crowd. "I'm Hermann Almstedt," he shouted. "It was my daughter who was attacked. And I beg of you, let this man get a fair trial."

Some in the crowd hissed. "Shut up," one of the thugs holding the rope called. "Or we'll lynch you too." The noise from the crowd grew louder.

Mr. Almstedt turned and vanished into the crowd.

Mr. Scott was truly abandoned.

"Summary justice! Summary justice!"

A shudder ran through my body. I jumped up on the railing. "No! Don't do this! You can't do this."

"Summary justice!"

"On behalf of your children," I called.

"Go back where you came from, you Communist kid." The growled voice was close by. Silas.

I found Silas's face in the crowd and addressed him. "Mr. Scott is innocent. Stop this lawlessness," I called out. "You'll regret it. The future will see you as losers."

Sneers and jeers greeted me.

"Set an example!" I cried.

"We're setting 'em an example, all right, kid. We'll lynch you too."

I stood on the railing, feet apart. They put the longer rope in place as a noose around Mr. Scott's neck.

"You have to stop!" I cried out.

Amid shouts, they lifted my friend to the railing next to me. And pushed us both off.

CHAPTER 33

He plunged beside me.

Branches whipped my face as I fell through the trees. In the blur I saw a face. Ned's face.

Then I landed with a thump and a roll in the snow at the foot of a hill in gathering dusk.

Alone. Mr. Scott was not with me.

On all fours, I felt waves of nausea and dizziness batter me. Mr. Scott must be dead.

I looked upward. The moon hung in the dusky stillness like nothing was wrong, nothing was different.

But it was.

Woods in winter. Nausea. Dizziness. My next reality.

I stumbled to my feet, feeling hollow inside. Somehow, I hadn't died. Or even been injured. Whether there were cedar trees in that ravine or there was some other key to time and space, it had been turned.

I looked down at what I was wearing: the overalls, shirt, cap, and boots that had belonged to Frederick McLaren. In the snow, these boots were a welcome change from sneakers. I needed my jacket but didn't have it. My ears tingled with the cold.

The terrible crime I'd witnessed played through my mind. The group of men and the townspeople, so determined to make a quick end of it. Laughing, honking. Unconcerned about justice and mercy. Treating it as a fun outing. Even, some of them, bringing their children along. I'd seen the face of evil, and it looked very human.

Loss overwhelmed me. Mr. Scott dead, and I hadn't been able to make a difference. I stood and shivered until my teeth chattered, head bowed. James Scott. My friend, might he rest in peace.

The cold forced me to move, and I began to circle the hill, walking fast. I needed to get my bearings.

Perhaps I was in 1969 again. Camping, but without any gear, my hat, or my jacket.

Morris. I'd been looking for Morris, still was. I had a message to deliver. Maybe Ned had put me down in a place where I could now find him.

I scuffed my foot in the thin, partly melted snow. It wasn't much of a snowstorm that had deposited this.

I took stock of my surroundings. Listening carefully, I heard no traffic sounds—I was too far from a road. Silhouetted against the darkening sky stood a structure at the top of the hill. There was a cabin up there.

Morris used to talk about finding one or building one.

I walked closer. It was falling apart. It had a roof made of sticks and thatch, but it didn't look like it could keep the rain out. Gaping darkness looked out of the holes that served as windows. A shiver ran up my spine.

From my spot just upwind, I crouched, cupped my hands behind my ears, and listened—for anything. I heard nothing.

I knelt to touch the remains of a fire in an outside fire ring. Cold. Stone cold. But still sooty.

Someone might have died in there.

I crept to the open doorway and peered in. Nothing moved, but the murky interior didn't let me pick out any details. I stood for a long moment and let my eyes adjust.

Off to one side, under a window, lay someone in a bedroll.

I couldn't tell if he was dead at first. Then I took a step into the cabin. "You okay?"

"Who's that?"

I knew the voice, disused as it was.

I knelt beside him. "Morris?"

He stirred, and then he groaned.

CHAPTER 34

"What's wrong?" I asked, reaching my hand toward him.

"Busted leg." Morris grunted. "Broke it yesterday." His breath came in gasps full of pain.

"What happened?"

"Went to get water. In the night." His voice had a hitch in it. "Snow stopped. Lots of light. From the moon. Got most of the way back." He stopped, took a deep breath, then continued. "Tripped. Fell down the hillside right outside here. Busted my leg. Took hours to drag myself ... up the hill."

I touched his shoulder. "It hurts?"

"It hurts bad."

Silence.

"You got a flashlight, Morris?" I started shivering as I stood.

"Next to the door. My pack. Got two flashlights. And a spare jacket. Take 'em."

I found the flashlights, handed one to him, and put on the coat. I could see him now as he pointed the light towards himself for my benefit.

Pain hitched his breath. He rolled to one side with a grunt and pulled an ornate silver pocket watch out of his pocket, shone the flashlight on it like a spotlight. "My grandad's," he said. "Got to make ... sure I didn't break it ... when I fell."

He motioned with his head toward a spot next to his pack where my flashlight picked out a pair of large, black boots. "New boots. Got 'em ... from the food pantry." He grimaced. "Too big. Made me trip."

I walked around the cabin, flicking my flashlight beam into all the corners. His stuff sat piled beside him, including his canteen. Other corners contained heaps of old leaves and sticks—animal nests from warmer weather.

"Find the jerky," he said. "Hung over a branch. Straight out the door. Down the hill."

I retrieved a big cloth bag. I also rummaged through his belongings and found acorns. We shared a meal, bathed in the glare from my flashlight. Chilly air drifted in through the windows. There'd be ice on the trail—it was below freezing.

"Morris," I said. "I went to town. I found out that Celia is still waiting for you, and the police aren't looking for you. Miss Anna told me to tell you this—you need to come back."

"Thanks ... for finding out." He lapsed into silence. "Say, Richie ... lost your ... stuff?"

"I tried to tell you once before," I said. "My plants book was published in 2019. This time I lost my stuff traveling. Time traveling."

He frowned, hitched his breath, and waved his hand in front of his face, as if gnats were gumming up his vision. "That don't ... make no sense."

"For the past week, I've been hanging out with your grandfather. The one who got lynched. I tried to prevent it, and I couldn't. But he died well," I said. "He didn't run."

"We go back to Shady Creek ... and those police goin' ... to catch you," he said. He gritted his teeth and shifted his position.

I leaned back. "I know. But you got to get back home. And I'm going to stop running now."

"You ... ain't got to do this ... just for me."

"Yes, I do. You've done so much for me. So, I want to do a little bit for you."

We lapsed into silence, overshadowed by pain.

I gathered wood from nearby, made a fire, melted some snow to drink, and fidgeted. I needed to keep myself warm without a bedroll. It was going to be a long night.

CHAPTER 35

With the daylight, a crisp cold wind blew in through the windows and doors of the homemade cabin. I stacked Morris's stuff in one corner. I hung the jerky again from the tree, in case somebody needed it. The only thing I'd take was his rifle, carefully unloaded so I could use it as a walking stick.

After I filled two canteens from the creek and draped them across my chest, I pulled Morris up on his one good foot. He stifled a cry. I put my left arm around his waist and let him cast his right arm around my shoulders. Then I gripped the gun barrel with my free hand and stabbed at the ground for balance with the other end. We set out, with Morris hopping and me supporting his heavier weight and taller frame at every step, an effort that tested all my strength.

Grim, gray clouds covered the sky.

Our pathway across the little hill was covered in a layer of snow, free of ice. Once we entered the woods, slick patches gave bad footing. Morris gasped for breath to deal with the pain. At one point we fell down, Morris cried out, and it took half an hour to get started again. He leaned more heavily on me, and we moved slower and slower.

It might have been noon when we struggled up the bank to the road. Sunlight poured through the clouds and picked out a distant green box truck moving towards us on the ribbon of highway. I took a deep breath and let it out. Ned was coming. "I know that guy," I said. "It's my friend, Ned. He drives that green truck. He writes haiku poems."

Ned was slowing down, and Morris dropped his head forward. "I hope we can get me in." His voice sounded faint.

Ned got out, wearing a brown uniform that said "Wizer's Delivery" on the sleeve. "Thought I might find you along about now." I smelled cinnamon. Strong this time.

"Man, I'm glad you're here," I said. Morris teetered on my shoulder.

Ned was strong, stronger than I thought. He grabbed Morris and boosted him in. Morris closed his eyes, grimaced, and groaned loudly. "I got to raise my leg." Ned and I positioned him sideways, leaning against the passenger-side door, legs across Ned's lap. I folded myself up on the floor, clutching my knees. I tore off my jacket as the heater blasted hot air on me.

Soon we were rumbling up the road.

"We'll go to St. Joseph's Hospital," said Ned.

Morris shifted his body and moaned.

The hospital was near Shady Creek. It would take at least two hours to get there. "Hang on, Morris." I patted the back of his hand.

Ned flicked on the radio. A hymn surged into the cab, rich with the sound of an organ, deep-toned music vibrating in the air. Morris stilled after a while and slept. My sleepless night dragged at my eyelids, but I fought it. I had so many questions.

"Ned, you gotta tell me how and why. About time traveling to 1923. About why I was there if I couldn't fix things. About seeing your face as I go through the gateways."

He shrugged. "Life can be really hard to explain."

"No kidding. So, you got superpowers or something?"

"What do you think?"

"I think you do."

He looked right at me and grinned, an impish twinkle in his eye.

I wasn't entirely happy with him. "I think you coulda helped me while I was in 1923. And other times too. But when I needed you, you weren't there."

He shook his head. "I might be able to help a little here and there, but it's not my journey—it's your own. You got to deal with what comes up."

"Hmmph." Not the answer I wanted.

Ned nodded toward Morris. "He saved you. You learned some things. And now he's going home. You did well."

"I suppose." But grief for James Scott sat in the pit of my stomach like an unchewed wad.

The organ music filled my ears, my head, my inner being, and I dropped my head against my knees. It was so hard to stay awake. I was so tired. I didn't even ask to hear the latest haiku.

The silence of the stilled truck engine woke me. We had pulled up to the emergency entrance to the hospital.

After that it was a flurry of activity as a team of medical people unloaded Morris from the truck cab onto a gurney. As they wheeled him into the ER, I grabbed Morris's gun by the stock and started to follow. Then I felt a warm hand on my shoulder.

"I'm taking off, Richie." Ned's voice sounded grave.

My breath caught. I was expecting it, but I wasn't ready.

"God bless you, son. You can take it from here." He turned to go.

I could? "Wait! Will I see you again?" I grasped after him fruitlessly, like somebody trying to catch a bird with one hand.

"I can't tell you," he said. Then he turned to leave.

Feeling empty, I followed Morris's gurney into the hospital.

CHAPTER 36

They put the gun in a locker and asked me a ton of questions about Morris and who his family was. Security asked where we'd lived in the woods. And about who I was. I told them my name, and they wrote it down.

I had a feeling the Farmington cop would soon find out about me, the kid who answered the description of the missing teenage car thief. My future did not look bright.

They asked had I used drugs. Had I abused alcohol. Why hadn't I notified my parents.

A nurse stuck her head into Morris's room. "You're waiting for Morris Scott, right?"

I looked at her, eyes heavy. "Yes, ma'am."

"You might want to go to the waiting room. His family is there now." She gave directions and left.

I made my way to find the others. I peeked in through the glass window beside the door. Miss Anna, Celia, and some others I didn't know stood in a corner talking. Miss Anna, Morris's aunt, was a teenager when I'd met her in 1923. Had I really been there?

As I entered the room, low voices reached my ears. "The doctor said the surgery would last three hours. It's been two."

I slumped into a chair beside the door.

"A friend of Deon's brought him back. White boy."

Footsteps approached me. A soft hand touched my shoulder. "Richie? That you, Richie?"

Celia threw an arm around my neck as I stood up. I tried to tell her I needed a bath, but she gave me a hug anyway.

"We all needed him back." She began telling me how the nightmare was over, that everything had worked out. "Mr. Eldridge, the old man who lost the silver teapot and accused Morris. They found the teapot, in somebody's compost heap, a few years ago."

Mr. Eldridge died last year, as it turned out. They just got his estate all settled recently and he'd actually left money to Morris. "Ten thousand dollars!" She danced on her tiptoes.

I needed to sit down before my knees gave way. Miss Anna said, "You done good," as she patted my hand. An idiot grin pasted on my face.

A businesslike silver-haired cop strode in, glanced around the room. His eyes came to rest on me. "Pete Hungerford?" His gravelly voice rasped like a wire brush cleaning a grill.

I climbed to my feet. Miss Anna and the others backed away. "Ah, no, sir. I'm Richard Roberts." It was reckoning time.

"I'm looking for Pete Hungerford, who was hanging out in the woods north of Farmington recently." He flashed his badge. "Trevor Humbert, Farmington PD."

"I was hanging out in the woods north of Farmington recently," I said. "I thought somebody was chasing me, but I am not Pete Hungerford."

"You got ID?"

"No, sir."

"Son, you left school here in Shady Creek, a truant suspected of stealing cars in Farmington. I knew about your troubles at home and was worried you'd take your own life, so I borrowed a dog. Couldn't catch you, though. But now, here you are." He shook his head. "It's time to go home, Pete."

I could tell him I hadn't left school because where I came from school was out for the summer. But he wouldn't believe me.

The door opened again, and a slender, middle-aged man with wire-rimmed glasses thrust himself into the room. He approached me, hesitating. "Pete?" He scrunched his eyes closed and reopened them, puzzlement in his face.

I shook my head.

The man turned to the cop. "This isn't my son, officer."

"You're kidding."

"No, sir. Looks like him, but isn't him."

"I'm not the one you're looking for, and it's time for me to leave." I pulled the door open and slipped out into the hall while they continued to argue.

I needed to go. But where?

Where was my place? Not beside Morris anymore. Not protecting Mr. Scott anymore. Not alone in the Ozark woods anymore.

In the hall, I found a hard metal chair and sat down on it.

CHAPTER 37

Then I knew. My place was in 2019— where I had a future. I'd come from there, and I'd go back.

Morris was still on the operating table, and I couldn't say goodbye. But I didn't know what I'd say, anyway. I'd see him again after he'd lived fifty more years, I already knew that.

I made my way out a door to the hospital grounds. There just had to be a gateway here somewhere. I stepped between two young trees, wondering if I'd find myself in some strange place or time. I glimpsed Ned's face again, and a wave of nausea hit me.

Clutching my head to stop the dizziness, I realized I was in my front yard. It was late afternoon and very warm, summertime warm. I stood behind Aunt Trudy as she bent over her rose bushes with clippers, wearing gloves. She was muttering to herself, "Gone three weeks. Seems like years."

She glanced up and saw me. "Richie? Richie, did you come back?" She dropped the roses and the shears and reached for me. For a hug. "I'm sorry, I'm so sorry," she murmured.

I felt stiff as a stick.

But she wasn't stiff. She gave a real genuine hug, the first I remembered from her.

She'd never apologized to me before.

Maybe things would be different now.

Or maybe they wouldn't.

She led me to the lawn chairs in the small back yard of the tiny ranch house. "Let's sit down and have a talk, Richie. It's time."

If I could shout down a mob, I could tell her what I thought. "I couldn't stand it here. You kept treating me like I was a little kid—not good at anything. Calling me names, like I'm a no-good idiot." I didn't expect sadness to get caught in my voice.

A tear trickled down her cheek. "I was in the library at the front desk the other day, and I saw a mother and her five-year-old. She was bringing books to turn in."

There was a new tone in her voice. I inched forward a bit to hear better.

"He was pulling away from her, wanting to run up the stairs to the children's department, couldn't wait to get there.

"You were older when I got you, Richie, but all the same, you did that, tried to pull away from me. I just pulled back and got mad. You weren't doing what I wanted, weren't obeying me. But that's not what she did. She dropped his hand. 'Go!' she said. 'I'll race you up there.'

"She was letting her little boy do what he really wanted to do. I followed her. And, sure enough, the boy brought her a book and asked her to read it to him. They curled up in a big chair in that children's library room, looking so cozy and close and ... I bet when he's fourteen she'll still be his friend." She wiped away tears.

I crossed my arms in front of my chest. The names she'd called me whispered through my head. Stupid, idiot ... I didn't want to remember them.

"I have failed you, Richie. My life was out of order when I was a kid, and all I wanted to do was get it under control.

"But when you ran away, I realized ... it wasn't worth it, controlling you. And I was hurting you. And me. I'm not going to do it anymore."

I had to remember what Dad said: "You can't run away from trouble. It'll always find you." Here she was, trouble for me.

But could she change? I had to believe she could. So many hurtful words had left scars on my soul, but I let her hug me again. This time, I felt a little less stiff.

Later, in the house, I stopped in front of a photograph in the hall, part of a large number of old photos she'd had framed. I'd hardly looked at them before, but this time one face caught my eye.

I pointed. "Who's that?"

"Oh, I think that's your great-great-grandfather," she said.

I felt like someone socked me in the gut.

"Yes, that's who it is."

My mind was not connecting.

"You okay?" Aunt Trudy asked, a frown creasing her face.

"He looks like ... I've seen him before."

"He was a Wilson. That was his name. Silas Wilson, I believe."

I wished she hadn't told me. I shouldn't have even asked.

"I think he lived down in Columbia."

She shouldn't have known the answer. I wished I didn't know. I didn't want to know anymore. I didn't want to know any of it.

"Yes, it was him. You get your love of cars from him, I think, someone on that side of the family."

She was trying to be nice.

"Silas Wilson," she said.

I didn't know how to seal it off. I couldn't stop it. The mob images ran through my head. The faces contorted with hate. The hoarse shouts. Mingled with them, Aunt Trudy's voice condemning me. "Idiot."

I retreated to my room and sat in the little folding chair next to the bed. I was shaking, gripping my head between my hands. The awful images and words kept hammering on me.

Then, for some reason, I looked up. On my pillow was a slip of paper. I picked it up. It was a scrawled note.

"Hear music playing
Filling heart and soul with peace,
Healing broken hearts."

A haiku from Ned. The organ chords I'd heard in his truck played in my head, rich and slow, pushing the other stuff away. It was like I'd stepped into some calm backwater in the river of time where there was comfort and healing—and the smell of cinnamon. The music soothed me, muted the horrible shouts and the harsh words, and then melted them away.

Finally, I stood up. All I could hear was my slow, regular heartbeat.

I had a feeling that living at home wouldn't be easy, that I'd need to step into Ned's music on a regular basis. But that's how it would have to be.

I reviewed what I'd learned, what I'd done. What I'd failed to do.

I'd found out I couldn't solve the past, at least James Scott's part of it.

But I'd solved another part. Morris had come in from the cold.

I'd allowed Aunt Trudy to see the error of her ways. And perhaps I'd somehow redeemed the awful actions of my great-great-grandfather.

And I'd learned to reach out, outside my comfort zone. I remembered my discomfort at meeting Morris, a black man. That was a long time ago, in so many ways.

I crossed to the black settlement on the north side of Shady Creek. Not only did the little neighborhood not feel dangerous to me now, but I felt comfortable there. It was the home of my friends.

With little difficulty, I located the small brick house where Miss Anna, Deon, and Sojo had lived so many years before. I wasn't surprised to see an old couple on the porch of the house next door, keeping cool in the evening air.

I approached. It was Celia and Morris, now in their eighties, shoulders stooped and faces wrinkled. Morris took a good look at me and broke into a broad grin. "Richie! I knew I'd be seeing you soon."

Celia stood and gave me a big hug. "Just glad we lived long enough," she whispered in my ear. Then she laughed, a ringing, glad laugh.

Morris pointed to his bum leg propped on a chair, motioned me over, and we shook hands. A nod passed between us.

"Fifty years is a long time to wait," he said. "You look bigger now. Bigger than I remember. Been getting better meals than rabbits and acorns, I think."

"Yeah." I leaned against a pillar of the porch. "Some nice folks in Columbia gave me a lot of chicken livers." I chuckled.

Celia scraped her chair on the floor. "If you'll excuse me, I need to go start dinner. You're staying, right, Richie?"

"Thanks, I'd love to."

I sat beside him. "You still got that pocket watch?"

He pulled a jumble of parts from his pocket, turning the case over and over in his hands.

"I'm gonna fix it for you," I said. "I'll get some mowing jobs and get the job done."

He shook his head. "You ain't got to do that, Richie."

"Of course, I will. I want to."

I told him more about my time with James Scott then, as a light breeze came up. Morris told me that no one was ever convicted of the college-town lynching, though it made the front page of the New York Times. Miss Gertrude never recovered from depression. But Harrison and Anna moved in with their uncle in Shady Creek and grew up here. As had he, of course.

I felt I had to tell him about my great-great-grandfather, and I apologized.

"You ain't responsible for what he did," Morris said, finally. "And you yourself did a lot there, even if you didn't succeed."

"I'm sorry. I'm so sorry, Morris."

"You're living with that mean aunt of yours."

"Yes. I think maybe she will be nicer now."

"Well, if she ain't, you just come on over here and stay with us."

I swallowed. "Thank you, Morris."

He got his cane and led me haltingly toward the house next door. "I got someone for you to meet," he said. "My grandson."

The door opened at his knock. "Pops!" called a voice. "What you doing over here? You ain't supposed to be off that porch." It was a guy about my age wearing a black tee shirt.

"LaDavid, I wanted you to meet my old friend," he said. "This here is Richie."

This was surely one of the three black teenagers I'd run away from when I broke Morris's pocket watch. I had a chance to do this over now—and fix what I could.

I shook LaDavid's hand vigorously. "I am truly pleased to meet you."

The End

FACT VS. FICTION

This novel contains a true story, the lynching of James T. Scott, custodian at the University of Missouri, in Columbia in 1923.

But in order to flesh out the story, I had to make up some things. So, what's not historical in the 1923 scenes?

Richie is fictional, along with the McLarens, the newsboys, and Silas Wilson.

The historical individuals include James T. Scott, his wife, his mother, his lawyers, his pastor, his brother in St. Louis, and the others associated with the attack on Regina Almstedt. Also historical were the mob leader, George Barkwell, as well as the journalism student, Charles Nutter, who provided an eyewitness account for the *Columbia Evening Missourian* and the *New York Times*.

James T. Scott had two or three children with his first wife in Chicago, but historians are unsure of their gender and their whereabouts at the time of the lynching. They also don't know what happened to them. I filled this gap with some fictional characters.

The night of the lynching was documented in the newspapers, and I drew on these accounts to describe the situation as it unfolded.

George Barkwell, mob leader, was eventually tried for murder but dodged the rap since only Charles Nutter would testify against him, while others testified in his favor.

ABOUT THE AUTHOR

Author Phyllis Wheeler has done a little bit of many things. After studying English in college she worked for five years as a newspaper reporter. Then she went back to school and became a mechanical engineer working in aerospace for seven years. As her family grew she took on her next career as a homeschool teacher. She created and self-published a computer-programming curriculum (focusing on fun projects for kids) that won first-place awards.

Eventually she picked up her childhood goal of writing a children's book and moved into the publishing world. With a friend she operated a small press for five years, winning several awards. Most recently she's been working hard on her own writing. She lives in St. Louis with her husband, keeping tabs occasionally on their four grown children. Find out more and get a free short story as well as a study guide for this book at PhyllisWheeler.com.

Kind reader, I would love your help getting the word out about this book. Please go to the place where you purchased the book and review it! And if you found the opportunity at the end of your e-book to rate it up to five stars, please be advised that this information doesn't go to the review section of the sales website and can't replace an actual review from you. Thank you so much for your help!

If you liked it, please also tell friends about it.

Keep in touch by signing up for my author newsletter at PhyllisWheeler.com, which is also where you can find discussion questions.

Made in the USA
Las Vegas, NV
02 June 2021